THE
DOWNSIDE
OF BEING UP

ALSO BY ALAN LAWRENCE SITOMER

Nerd Girls

The Secret Story of Sonia Rodriguez

Homeboyz

Hip-Hop High School

The Hoopster

THE DOWNSIDE OF BEING UP

ALAN LAWRENCE SITOMER

G. P. PUTNAM'S SONS
AN IMPRINT OF PENGUIN GROUP (USA) INC.

G. P. PUTNAM'S SONS • A division of Penguin Young Readers Group.
Published by The Penguin Group.

Penguin Group (USA) Inc., 375 Hudson Street, New York, NY 10014, U.S.A.
Penguin Group (Canada), 90 Eglinton Avenue East, Suite 700, Toronto, Ontario
M4P 2Y3, Canada (a division of Pearson Penguin Canada Inc.).
Penguin Books Ltd, 80 Strand, London WC2R ORL, England.
Penguin Ireland, 25 St. Stephen's Green, Dublin 2, Ireland
(a division of Penguin Books Ltd.).
Penguin Group (Australia), 250 Camberwell Road, Camberwell, Victoria 3124,
Australia (a division of Pearson Australia Group Pty Ltd).
Penguin Books India Pvt Ltd, 11 Community Centre,
Panchsheel Park, New Delhi—110 017, India.
Penguin Group (NZ), 67 Apollo Drive, Rosedale, North Shore 0632,
New Zealand (a division of Pearson New Zealand Ltd).
Penguin Books (South Africa) (Pty) Ltd, 24 Sturdee Avenue,
Rosebank, Johannesburg 2196, South Africa.
Penguin Books Ltd, Registered Offices: 80 Strand, London WC2R ORL, England.

Published simultaneously in Canada. Printed in the United States of America.
Design by Annie Ericsson.
Text set in Matt Antique BT.

Library of Congress Cataloging-in-Publication Data
Sitomer, Alan Lawrence.
The downside of being up / Alan Lawrence Sitomer.
p.   cm.
Summary: All Bobby Connor wants is to survive middle school, but puberty is making that
difficult for him as his body conspires against him.
[1. Penis—Fiction. 2. Middle schools—Fiction. 3. Schools—Fiction. 4. Interpersonal
relations—Fiction. 5. Family life—Fiction. 6. Humorous stories.] I. Title.
PZ7.S6228Do 2011
[Fic]—dc22   2010044203

ISBN 978-0-399-25498-7
10 9 8 7 6 5 4 3 2 1

For guys everywhere who get it.
And girls everywhere that don't.

1

Look, I'm just a kid. I'm not a dork, a jock, a brain, a freak or a perv. I like cheeseburgers with ketchup, video games and movies. No, I'm not the most popular student in school, yes, I am toilet trained, and okay, once in a while I pick my nose. Also, I like baseball.

But I have absolutely no control over what goes on in my pants. I get eighteen boners a day.

Literally.

I get them when I'm emptying the dishwasher. I get them when I'm putting on socks. I get them when I'm in the cereal section of the supermarket. Why would cereal straighten my weinerschnitzel? Really, I have no idea. It just pops up out of nowhere. And when I say pop I mean *pop!* It's like having a steel pole rise in my pants.

Not a very big pole, though. I've measured. Right now it's four and five-eighths inches long. Let's just say I've already prayed to the penis gods and offered 'em a trade. I told them I'd swap my left pinkie toe for an extra two and one-eighths inches of manhood. That would bring me close to seven. Pretty fair exchange, right? Sure, I may limp for the rest of my life, but at least I'd be packing a bit of thunder. I mean right now I don't even have a rain cloud in my jeans. On the naked self-esteem scale I score a negative ninety-three.

Holy cow, I don't even know why I'm talking about all this. Actually, I do. It's because no one ever discusses this stuff. It's like some sort of sweep-it-under-the-rug topic that no one ever talks about even though all guys go through it. I mean, the closest anyone ever comes to even mentioning it is in sex education class, except in there all they do is show pictures of limp penises (or penii, whatever you call them) and they're always attached to an inner gland or something. *Barf!!* Is there anything on the planet less attractive than a side-view medical diagram of a soft beef kabob? Really, just shoot me right now.

Basically, I get stiffies all the time for absolutely no reason and they are ruining my life.

Seriously, I want them to stop.

But they don't, or won't, so I'm forced to hide them. Oversized shirts that I wear untucked. Baggy pants with enough room inside the crotch for a microwave oven. Dictionaries I keep on my lap as if I am eager to look up fourteen-letter vocabulary words just for the "exuberating experience of exponentially enhancing my grandiloquent education."

Yeah, right. The only thing a big ol' *Webster's* is good for to a kid like me is hiding my ding-dong when it stands at full attention. Fact is, my wang has completely flipped its wong and though I'm not sure when it happened, successfully hiding my boners has become the greatest battle of my life.

Yet, one time I failed. I blew it. I got busted with a sky-high pork pipe. That's what forced me into "correctional erectional analysis." Yep, therapy. A shrink. Writing about it is supposed to help. At least that's what my therapist says. My second therapist, that is. My first therapist, well, let's just say that my correctional erectional analysis seems to have sent her zooming into some sort of psychotic midlife crisis of her own . . . but her meltdown's another story.

Really, this is my last chance. I just hope that scribbling down the hard truth about my out-of-control bologna pony is going to allow me to get a grip on life and move on.

It's cruel. It's torturous. It's Bonerville Middle

School, a place where all red-blooded boys eventually have to go.

And it ain't no fun. It ain't no fun at all.

Especially when ya, you know, kinda like a girl.

2

There's only one person in the entire world I know who would bring a cockroach to math class and think it's cool.

Alfred Finkelstein.

I hate Alfred Finkelstein. I hate his pimply skin. I hate his snorting laugh. I hate the fact that his parents took him to the cheapest orthodontist in the city for braces and allowed his mouth to be filled with enough metal to build a warship. If someone holds up a giant magnet, Alfred Finkelstein's face is going to get sucked across the room like a piece of lint being slurped up by a Godzilla-size vacuum cleaner.

Worst of all, though, is that Alfred Finkelstein is one of those kids who needs to add a dash of sexy flavor to his orthodontic madness. Now sure, lots of kids these days get color choices, but regular kids choose red or blue or pink. Finkelstein's cheapo orthodontist only offers second- and third-level choices, like "vomit green" or "diarrhea brown" or "urine yellow." This week Finkelstein is wearing the color "dog-poop up-chuck" on his teeth. I swear I can't tell where the food he ate for breakfast that got stuck in his metal grill begins and the dental design Dr. Dento Demento has provided him with ends. When Finkelstein smiles, I want to gag.

"Hey, Bobby," Finkelstein said, holding his new best friend in his hand. "Check it out. I put a booger on the back of this cockroach and he's carrying it around like a backpack."

I turned and saw a chunky green boulder sitting on the back of a one-inch brown roach. Immediately, I wanted to yak.

"Wanna see him do the booger boogie? I trained this sucka to dance."

"Get away from me, Finkelstein. And don't touch me, you freak!"

Finkelstein snorted a laugh—"he-hurrggh, he-hurrggh"—and then affectionately petted the back of his cockroach like it was some kind of fluffy kitten. It scares me to think that one day Finkelstein is going to become an adult with a job, a car and his own place to live. There should be a law in the United States that ships putzes like Finkelstein off to a farm to drink the milk of cloned goats or something, to see if there will be adverse effects on the rest of civilization. At least that would put his existence to some sort of productive use because right now, Alfred Finkelstein is an outright waste of human flesh.

"Okay, class. Turn to the next page on fractions and decimals," came the no-nonsense voice of our math teacher from the front of the room.

"Get down . . . Boogie-oogie-oogie. Get down . . . ," Finkelstein sang from his desk behind me, still playing with his cockroach.

"Shut up, Finkelstein. You're gonna get me in trouble like yesterday."

"Takes two to talk in class, Bobby."

"That's why I'm sayin' shut up, Finkelstein." Jeez, was he mentally incapacitated? Sometimes it felt like the city of Bonnerville had an idiot factory and all their reject samples ended up as kids on our campus, with Finkelstein being their number one moronic product.

I looked at the front board and tried to see what riveting thing we'd be doing today.

Oh, look, numerators and denominators. What joy.

My math class was taught by the oldest, dustiest, most crustiest teacher ever, Mrs. Mank. I think she taught my mom, my mom's mom, and even the mom of my mom's mom. During her first year as a teacher, schools didn't use chalkboards; they used abacuses. Mrs. Mank was old like protoplasm.

"Jenny Stoops, please go to the board and solve equation number one."

I turned the page in my textbook and *Uh-oh* . . .

No. Please, no, I thought. There was absolutely no reason for it. *Noooo.*

I tried to make it go away. I thought about baseball. I thought about canary birds. I thought about earwax and the armpits of old people and toe cheese.

No luck. It was Boner Time!

"Please, go away," I said. However, my south-of-the-border sausage salami had a mind all its own. Seems that Mrs. Mank's mathematical conversion from fractions to decimals had set it off. And I was wearing thin, white Nike track pants, too, the worst possible boner-hiding outfit ever.

So stupid. Why did I even buy these things? I mean, looking cool for school is one thing, but sporting uncontrollable wood is completely something else.

I gazed down at the tent I was pitching in my pants. Really, sometimes my brain freezes like when you drink a slushie too fast.

I slowly moved my math book off of my desk and onto my lap, then checked around to make sure no one was looking.

Coast was clear.

But this rod was a mean one. How come a guy's downtown equipment didn't come with an off button or something? Like was that a design oversight? It just doesn't make any sense that these things appear out of nowhere all the time for no good reason whatsoever. Someone needs to invent a pill or something.

"No, that's not how you do it, Jenny. Remember how we talked about moving the decimal point over two spaces?" Mrs. Mank showed Jenny the correct way to solve the equation and then turned back to the class to select the next volunteer. "Michael Demmings, you're up. Please come to the board and solve problem number two."

Michael went to the board. I felt relieved. Since Michael sat one row over from me, the next person Mrs. Mank would call would come from the other side of the room. When it came to board work, teachers never called on people from the same side of class. They liked to spread the pain around.

"Oh, this is not that hard," Mrs. Mank said in a frustrated voice as Michael screwed up problem number two. "Bobby Connor, please come to the board and show us how to solve equation number three."

"Me?" I said. Secretly, I reached under the book in my lap. Hard as a golf club.

"Yes, you," Mrs. Mank answered.

"Um . . . ," I replied. *Go down, go down,* I told my Popsicle. *Go down.*

Nothing. My banana was still hard enough to dent a door.

"Let's go, Bobby, hurry up," she said. "I have a lot of material to get through this week."

"Um . . . I don't know how to solve it, either, Mrs. Mank."

"Bobby Connor, you know as well as I do that this is simple stuff. Now, please come to the board and show us your mathematical abilities."

"Look, Teach, if I come to the board, I am going to show you a whole lot more than just my mathematical abilities."

Well, I didn't say that, but I was thinking it.

I paused. *What to do, what to do?*

"Bobby!" she snapped. "Get up here right now and stop wasting my time."

I didn't budge. She glared. Kids in the front started to turn around to see what was the matter with me.

With a boner like this, it would take a whole football team to drag me from my desk. No way was I standing up. No way at all.

Just then, I had the biggest stroke of luck ever.

"I think I know how to do it, Mrs. Mank," said Donnie Daniels, raising his hand. "Can I try?"

Donnie "Dipstick" Daniels was the dumbest kid in school. His skills were so bad that the Fs he got on his report card were actually higher marks than he had really earned. He was a Z student. Donnie didn't just fail regular classes like science and history; Donnie flunked lunch. Essentially, this meant that if Donnie was volunteering to go to the board to solve a math problem, there wasn't a teacher on the planet who was gonna stop him.

"Okay, Donald," Mrs. Mank said, still glaring at me. "Come on up." I looked at the clock on the wall. With only four more minutes until the bell rang, I was in the clear. I'd been saved by Donnie Dipstick.

Suddenly I felt a tickle on my neck. An itch of some sort. I reached up and scratched. A moment later something fell lightly into my lap.

I looked down. Finkelstein's booger roach was crawling up my leg.

"Aaarrgggh!" I screamed, leaping out of my seat.

Ew. Yuck. Eeee!! I jumped up and down and shook and twitched and wiggled and screamed. The cockroach flew into the air and then landed on the gray tile floor. It started to crawl away. I raised my foot and smashed it.

And smashed and smashed and smashed!

Everyone looked at me like I was nutso. Then their eyes slowly rotated from looking at the crazy expression on my face to looking down at the center of my white Nike track pants.

Nathan Ox, the class numb-nuts, was the first to speak.

"Look, everybody, Bobby's got a boner!"

Every eye in the room stared at my crotch.

"And it's only the size of a crayon!"

Bahhhh-hahahaha!! A huge shriek of laughter exploded from the room.

"What in the world is all the commotion? Now sit down, Bobby, and . . . *Aarrggh!*" Mrs. Mank suddenly screamed. My erection had surprised my math teacher so much that it caused her to fall backward, trip over a garbage can, bang her head against the board, collapse forward onto a chair, then slam to the floor.

Holy cow! I'd never seen an old lady take such a fall.

"Urrgghh," she groaned.

The class, of course, laughed harder than any other class in the history of school. Watching Mrs.

Mank bonk around like a human pinball was obviously the most hysterical thing they had ever seen.

Right then I knew I had to get out of there. I mean, even the quiet girls, the ones who never even dared chew a piece of bubble gum, were pointing at my pants with tears of laughter flowing from their eyes. I grabbed my backpack, bent over at the waist and dashed for the door.

Then I ran.

And ran.

I ran through the halls, I ran out of the building, I ran past two students who were hanging a large purple banner on the outdoor bulletin board advertising the traditional Big Dance that our school held every spring, and I didn't stop running until I was at the front gate of campus.

"Hey, you!" came a booming voice just as I was getting ready to sneak off of campus by crossing through the teachers' parking lot. "Where do you think you're going?"

Before I knew it, Mr. Hildge, the meanest, nastiest, rudest, most kid-hating vice principal that ever lived, stormed up to me with a walkie-talkie in one hand and a bullhorn in the other. His neck was thick like a tree trunk.

"I said, where do you think you're going?" He grabbed me with his bear-size hands.

Suddenly, his walkie-talkie crackled with life. *"Code green! Code green! We have a teacher down in the math department. Code green!"*

Life as I knew it was over.

3

"Oh my goodness, what are the neighbors going to think?"

Those were the first words out of my mother's mouth when I got home. She didn't ask how I was feeling. She didn't care if I was injured. She didn't want to know if I had suffered any permanent psychological trauma from having the most moronic kid in school tell the whole world my corncob was only the size of a crayon. All she cared about was one thing: "What are the neighbors going to think?"

Turns out, our school had an official policy against boners. And as my mother was notified when she came to pick me up, I had committed a violation of the Student's Code of Conduct item 84BLV.17: the "no parading of erections" clause in the student handbook that no one ever reads.

"No parading of erections? Hmmft," said my grandpa Ralph, wearing blue pajama pants and a white T-shirt with browning pit stains. "When I was

15

a kid, we were so broke we couldn't afford rulers, so our math teachers encouraged the boys to get pipes in our pants so that we'd at least have a way of drawing straight lines."

"Not helpful, Grandpa," my mom said in response. "This mister is in big trouble. Big trouble."

Mom stared angrily. I looked down.

Just then, my younger sister, Hillary, stormed through the front door.

"I hate you, Bobby!" she shouted as she slammed down her backpack. Hill was in seventh grade; I was in eighth. "I hate you even more than I used to hate you. I mean, do you realize that everyone's teasing me and making fun? You've ruined my life! Again!"

"Oh, honey," said my mother, trying to comfort her. Hill had been through a lot this past year with her accident and all, and she absolutely hated being in seventh grade. "I'm sure it can't be that bad."

"Oh yeah?" Hill replied. "The Spanish kids are calling me 'Lil' Hermana Ding-dong.'"

It took a moment for my mother to do the translation. Suddenly, her deep anger shifted to deep concern.

About what the neighbors would think, of course. To the left lived the Barkers. My mother wouldn't be too concerned about them, because their son Eddie once put a Fourth of July firecracker up their dog's butt and now they have to walk a pet that has no hair on its rear end. When Petey goes poo, it's like watching an alien spit out a Tootsie Roll. Not pretty at all.

But the Holstons, on the other hand—the neighbors on the other side—my mother was absolutely cuckoo about being better than them. She'd gone bonkers with the whole idea of it.

When the Holstons got a new car, we needed a new car. When the Holstons had their front lawn relandscaped, we had to have our front lawn relandscaped. When the Holstons got a pool, we needed to get a pool.

And when we didn't get a pool because we couldn't afford a pool, my mother decided to make her children better than their children. That was seven months ago. In the time since, my sister has been enrolled in ballet class, science academy and some junior lawyers of tomorrow organization. Me, I was bought a cello, a physicist starter set and a kit on human genomes.

Using the physicist materials, I accidentally set fire to the cello while my sister twirled the wrong way every eight minutes back at ballet class. Let's just say that none of my mom's plans to make her kids into supergeniuses worked out too well. And the Holstons still had their pool. Now this.

"Can we move?" Hill asked.

"Yeah, can we?" I added. Leaving town seemed like a great idea. "I can be packed in an hour."

"Shut up, Bobby," Hill snapped. "If we move, you're not coming. You've already destroyed enough of my existence in this lifetime." Hill turned back to our mother. "Please, Mom? I mean, they had to take Mrs. Mank out on a stretcher and all the kids are telling their parents she was attacked by Bobby Connor's puny baby boner. It's like some sort of tongue twister they're chanting around school." My sister started to imitate our school's new theme song. "Bobby Connor's Puny Baby Boner. Bobby Connor's Puny Baby Boner. Bobby Connor's Puny Baby Boner! Try saying that three times fast."

I paused and thought about it.

"She's right," I said to my mother, who stared blankly off into space. "We have to move."

"Shut your face, Bobby!" Hill yelled again.

My mother sat worriedly in a chair.

"Oh my goodness," she said, more to herself than to any of us. "My goodness."

"Maybe the boy just likes math," Grandpa Ralph

said, coming to my defense. "Like he *really* likes math. So much so that long division arouses his pickle?"

I gave Grandpa Ralph a "What the heck are you talkin' about" look. He smiled at me with crooked teeth and popped a purple jelly bean into his mouth.

"Just wait till your father comes home," my mom said. "Just wait, young man."

And sure enough, as if she had my dad on a string, a moment later his car pulled into the driveway. I gulped as my father, brown shoes, striped tie, white shirt, tan jacket over his shoulder, walked through the front door.

"So, what's up?" he said.

"Bobby was," answered Gramps. "But not very high."

"Huh?"

My dad scanned the room, clearly sensing the tension.

"Let's put it this way," Grandpa Ralph said. "Pork is on the dinner menu, and from what I hear, there ain't very much of it."

"Not helpful, Gramps," Mom said, shooting her father-in-law a look. Grandpa Ralph grinned at me and popped another jelly bean in his mouth. This time, green.

"We have a situation, Phillip," Mom announced, and then she kinda nodded in my direction.

Dad slowly turned. "Okay, what'd you do, Bobby?"

"Nothin'," I said.

"Nothing other than ruin my life," Hill added. "Again!"

"I didn't ruin your life," I said. "Last year wasn't my fault."

"'Last year wasn't my fault,'" she mocked in a high-pitched voice. "'I'm just innocent little Bobby, who only thinks about himself and never does anything wrong.'"

"Shut up, Hill," I said. "It wasn't my fault you missed all that school."

"'It wasn't my fault,'" Hill repeated.

"Stop it! The two of you," Mom ordered. She turned to Dad and explained. "Bobby paraded an erection in math class, which caused his teacher to fall and get sent to the hospital."

"He did what?" Dad exclaimed.

"He paraded an erection," Mom repeated.

My father struggled to fully understand what had happened.

"You hit your teacher with your penis?" he asked me.

"Phillip!" Mom snapped.

"What? I don't understand."

"Well, don't use the P-word."

"Why not? You used the E-word."

"The E-word is not the same as the P-word."

"It is too. The P-word and the E-word are the same thing," Dad said. "Now if I used an X-word or a double X-word, I could understand why you might have a problem, but the P-word, like the E-word, is perfectly acceptable."

"What the F-word are you two talking about?" asked Grandpa Ralph.

Mom turned. "Not helping, Gramps."

My grandfather grinned, popped a yellow jelly bean into his chompers and gave me a wink.

"I didn't do it on purpose, ya know!"

The house fell quiet at my outburst.

"Excuse me?" Mom said.

"I said . . . I didn't do it on purpose. It just, well, happened."

Mom started to nod her head. Slowly up, then slowly down. "Uh-huh," she said.

Compared to this, I was sure that having to walk a dog with no butt hair wasn't looking so bad to her after all.

"Can I be excused?" I asked in a low voice.

"I don't know, can you?" Mom said.

"Aw, let him go," Gramps piped in. "Maybe he needs to masturbate."

"I don't need to masturbate," I answered. For years I'd suspected that Gramps had some kind of mental disease or a steel plate in his head or a brain tumor. I mean, there had to be some sort of medical explanation for his loony behavior.

"No need to be ashamed, son," Gramps said. "All boys choke the chicken."

"Eww!" Hill looked at me like I was some kind of freak.

"You know, when I was a kid, we didn't have video games. This was my joystick right here," Gramps said, pointing to his pecker. "I used to play my skin flute till there were calluses on my hands."

"Okay," Hill said to no one in particular. "I'm officially running away."

"I say let the boy tug his pug if he needs to," said Gramps. "It's healthy, like vegetables."

"When is Grandpa Ralph going home?" I asked my parents.

"A few more days," Gramps replied, casually popping another jelly bean into his mouth. "A few more days."

"Well, does he have to sleep in my room? He snores and farts," I said.

"You, mister, are in no position to be complaining. I mean, think of the shame you have brought on this family," Mom said. "Phillip, say something to your son."

"What do you want me to say, Ilene? I mean, I still don't understand how he knocked his teacher over with his P-word. How big is this thing?"

"Rumor is, not very," Gramps answered.

"Not helping, Gramps," Mom said, trying not to flip out. She smoothed out her red blouse and made sure the green charm she wore on her gold necklace was in the exact center of her chest. Fixing her necklace was kind of a nervous habit of hers. "You are not helping at all."

Just then, the phone rang. Mom answered, happy to end the current conversation.

"Hello? Yes, Mr. Hildge . . ."

It was my school. Everyone got silent.

"Yes, I see . . . ," she said.

Mom listened some more.

"Uh-huh . . . uh-huh."

We all waited for information.

"I see. . . . Okay. . . . But you know he . . ." She stopped. "But he . . . but . . ."

My mother then listened for what felt like forever to me. What was going on? I wondered.

"Okay," Mom finally said. "I see. . . . Thank you for calling."

She hung up and looked around. All of us—my dad, my sister, Gramps—waited for the news.

"The charges have been elevated from parading to flaunting."

"Huh?" Dad asked. "What's that mean?"

"It means," my mother answered, shooting laser beams at me, "Bobby is being expelled."

"Expelled?" I gasped.

"For a boner?" exclaimed Gramps.

I couldn't believe it.

"For a stiffy?" Gramps continued. "For sporting a little wood with the ol' bologna bomb? For letting the Eiffel Tower shine some light on the city of Paris? For—"

"We get your point, Gramps," Mom said. "We get your point."

Gramps smiled mischievously. He seemed to greatly enjoy getting on my mother's last nerve. Me, I was more concerned with the phone call.

Apparently, parading was a misdemeanor. Flaunting was a felony.

"Ah, that school's crazy," Gramps added, tossing another jelly bean into his mouth. "If they throw every boy who's got a stiff salami in their trousers out of class, it'll be an all-girls school before the weekend. That ruling won't stick."

My feet felt like they were glued to the ground. I just stood there in shock. Despite what Gramps said, I was being bounced out of middle school.

My crime: erection-itis.

4

My dad works as an insurance claims adjuster. That means he considers himself a master negotiator. People smash up their cars, and instead of giving them five hundred bucks for their bumper my father will work 'em down to two-fifty. Frankly, he's outta control. It started last summer when he took some kind of become-a-millionaire-deal-maker seminar. Everything he's done since then in all aspects of his life has become a negotiation. Like, if I want a cheeseburger with fries, he'll say, "You can have a burger with cheese or a burger with fries, but you cannot have a burger with cheese and fries. Make your play."

I swear, that conference knocked a screw loose. It's gotten so bad around my house that for Valentine's Day he told my mom she could have either a bouquet of flowers or a box of chocolates, but he was not giving her both a bouquet of flowers and a box of chocolates.

"Make your play, Ilene."

From February fourteenth through February eighteenth Dad slept on the couch.

Anyway, that's how I avoided being expelled from school. My dad "negotiated" my return.

"Tell us how you did it, dear," Mom said, smiling. My mother was so tickled by my dad's deal-making triumph, she decided to cook his favorite dinner, Salisbury steak.

"The key to negotiation," Dad said as he proudly swirled a piece of brown meat in a glop of gravy, "is that you always need to know what the other person wants."

"You are so smart, honey," Mom said, putting more au gratin potatoes on his white plate.

"But they had me in a tight place on this one. I mean, they knew what I wanted. I wanted my son to be able to return to school. The key was figuring out what they wanted."

"And what did they want, dear?" Mom asked with a gleam in her eyes.

"Well, basically, they wanted to hear me admit my kid was a freak. A sick, depraved oddball. A disillusioned juvenile delinquent with highly deficient mental capabilities."

"Excuse me?" I coughed.

"See, I had to get them to think," Dad continued,

"that you were a pathetic, abnormal, semi-bizarre social outcast so that they'd take the bait."

"What?" I said.

"It's true," Hill said. "Every word."

"Shut up, Hill!"

"You shut up, Bobby."

"No, you shut up, Hill."

"Wow, you really stood up for your son there, huh, Phillip?" Gramps said, interrupting the intelligent conversation I was having with my sister.

"He's back at school, isn't he, Pop?" Dad replied sharply.

"Well, ya got me there, Father of the Year."

"You should talk," Dad replied.

Those two, my dad and my grandfather, had issues between them that dated back to long before I was born. My grandma, who was on some kind of cruise or something with her friends—and without Gramps, which is why he was here—told me a bunch of times about how those two never got along. Every holiday, birthday party or family event, they'd always argue with each other. Ruined the mood every time.

"What's this about bait?" I said, going back to the main discussion. Knowing my dad, there had to be some kind of catch to all this.

"Oh, this is the best part." Dad dunked a piece of

biscuit in the steak juice. "So I said to this Mr. Hildge guy, you can either show this child your compassion or you can show him your anger. Make your play."

My dad paused for effect like he had just spoken the ultimate quotable phrase.

"Make your play," he repeated, and then he plunked another triumphant chunk of Salisbury steak into his mouth.

"And that's it?" my mother asked.

"That's it. They took the bait. Bobby gets to go back to school tomorrow. No harm, no foul. Only one day out of class, just like he had a small fever or something."

I looked up, skeptical. It seemed too easy.

Dad swallowed his meat and then chugged a gulp of root beer. "All they made me do was sign some silly letter promising that you'd see the school psychologist."

"A shrink?" Mom asked, suddenly alarmed.

"For his dink?" Grandpa added. I turned to look at him. He grinned.

"When is Gramps going home?" I asked.

"A few more days," my grandfather answered, even though I wasn't talking to him.

Dad burped. "Don't worry, don't worry," my father said. He could tell the thought of me seeing a psychologist was very disturbing to Mom. "The school just hired a specialist who is well trained in issues surrounding adolescence and puberty. Bobby will be getting what's known as correctional erectional therapy."

"Correctional erectional therapy?" repeated my mother. An even greater look of concern flashed across her face. Everyone in the room could read her forehead as if it were a billboard.

What will the neighbors think?

Mom checked her necklace to make sure that the charm, some kind of red, oval-shaped thing, was perfectly centered. It was jewelry-fiddling time.

"Relax, honey, she's a professional," Dad said.

"I'm not going," I blurted out.

"Oh yes you are," Dad answered.

"Oh no I'm not," I said.

"Bobby," my father told me. "You can either go see this dink shrink and do your correctional erectional therapy like a man, or you can stay home with your grandpa Ralph doing chores until we find a new school to enroll you in. Make your play."

"No-brainer," I said. "I'll take the chores."

"Okay, chore number one is to go help your grandfather clean out his belly button."

"Is it the second Thursday of the month already?"

Gramps asked, his white hair shooting in all kinds of kooky directions, not having been combed for days. Gramps reached down, lifted his white T-shirt and looked at his stomach. "Sure is," he answered. "My, how quickly that gunk builds up in there." He turned to me. "Don't worry, I'll just need you to spread my navel while I extract the mucus. The tweezers'll get most of the creamy ooze out, but I gotta warn you, bring something to cover your nose. It ain't rosebushes growing down there."

Gramps offered me a crooked smile. I looked at my dad. He stared back at me like Dirty Harry.

"Make your play, Bobby. Make your play."

5

School the next morning wasn't nearly as bad as I thought it would be. The first person I saw after my mom dropped me off was a girl, a blonde, someone I had never seen before. I expected her to laugh in my face. Instead she said hi.

"Hi," I responded.

We locked eyes. Hers were green, like jewels.

A moment later, with another nice smile, she walked on and went inside.

Who was that? I thought.

Just then, I realized it had been over forty hours since the "incident" had happened. Maybe everyone had forgotten about it? I mean, so what, I had an erection. All boys get them. And after all, kids do have pretty short attention spans. I bet everyone had probably moved on to thinking about something else.

I took two steps forward, then ran into Nathan Ox. He wore a striped blue, red and green shirt that made him look like a human roll of Life Savers candy. His shirt was also so tight everyone could see his boy-boobs. Essentially, Nathan had a bigger set of water-melons than half the girls on campus. However, he'd wallop any kid who told him so.

"Hey, look who's back," Nathan called out. "It's boner face Bobby Connor!" Then he punched me in the coconuts. Nathan Ox was not just the class jerk-wad, he was also the class bully. And when he beat people up, he always went for a person's privates. Nut shots, pecker pounders—Nathan Ox thought groin pulverization was funny. "You gonna show Mrs. Baxter your wanker in science today, pecker face?"

A circle of kids, most all of them wearing back-packs, gathered to laugh at me. Nathan then took another punch at my acorns, but I lifted my knee so he only hit my thigh. Quickly, I broke through the circle, zipped across the grass by the flower bed no one was ever supposed to walk through and made a plan to avoid all human contact for the rest of my life.

It was at this moment that I realized there's sim-ply no group of people on the planet meaner than kids my age. Not jail wardens, not dictators, not even angry nuns. Middle school kids are the worst.

All day long people at school teased me, punched me, pointed at me and told stupid jokes about me. And it wasn't just the bullies who were picking on me, either. Total doofwads, kids who had been nerds and punks their whole lives, suddenly thought they could now start taking their shots, too.

"Hey, Bobby," said Chris Mickels from across the hall. "Is that a pencil in your pocket, or do you just wanna hump a four-hundred-year-old math teacher?"

Thwap! He nailed me with a spitball. Three girls giggled at the wad of saliva-soaked notebook paper sticking to my neck.

It's one thing to get picked on by a bully. It's something totally different to get picked on by a four-eyed, pimple-faced, asthmatic string bean. And it went on like this all day. Ordinarily, I would have punched Chris Mickels in the head and then shoved a spitball the size of a coffee cup down his throat, but I knew that if I caused any trouble, especially on my first day back, Mr. Hildge would have thrown me out of school quicker than a fat lady could eat an entire tray of brownies. And Chris knew this, too. That's why he felt so brave.

By the middle of the day, I realized none of my so-called friends were going to associate with me, either. Timmy Three-Nips, a kid with a third nipple who I'd saved from humiliation last year by volunteering to change sides in a PE game of shirts-versus-skins basketball, totally ignored me. Johnny Markano, a kid whom I'd informed that his fly was down before he gave his "My Dream Job" speech in sixth grade social studies, acted like he'd never seen me before in his life. And Anthony Leon pretended as if I hadn't let him come over for two weeks to play video games at my house when his parents took away every electrical gadget he owned for trying to put his baby sister's hair into a pencil sharpener.

Talk about being left hanging. Everything was against me. Even the school lunch menu.

"Hey, dingle nuts," Nathan said to me in the cafeteria line. "Today we're having hot dogs. Do you know the difference between a hot dog and a wiener?"

Fifty people stared at me waiting for the punch line to this obviously not-going-to-be-very-funny-to-me joke. "No, Nathan. What?"

"Well, in your case, about four inches and a whole lot of firmness," Nathan blurted out. Then he tried to shove a hot dog bun up my butt.

As Nathan did so, I looked to the school lunch lady for help. She wore a white uniform, white shoes and silly white hairnet thing.

Our lunch lady just giggled and watched Nathan torture me.

Wasn't she some kind of school employee who was supposed to intervene against bullying or something?

With flakes of hot dog bun hanging from my rear end, I crossed the gray-walled cafeteria and made my way past rows and rows of plastic yellow tables until I finally found a spot in the far corner of the lunchroom by a fire extinguisher that hung on the wall.

Lunch was usually smiles, food, chatter and people. Today, I was alone in the back corner of a windowless room, just me and my weenie.

"You know you're pathetic when even the lunch lady is laughing at you. *He-hurrggh, he-hurrggh.*"

"Shut up, Finkelstein."

"Oh, come on, bro. Don't let it be like that, I'm just messin'."

Clank! He set down his tray of food.

"Wanna hear my English-class poem?"

"No."

"Aren't you gonna ask what poem?" he asked.

"No," I said again.

"While you were out yesterday, we were assigned a poem for English. Everyone has to write one or they won't pass for the quarter. I call this one 'Zits.'"

"Don't read me your poem, Finkelstein."

"Zits," he began.

A sign of my maturity
A sign of my grace

A sign of adolescence
They cover my whole face
I squeeze them when they're juicy
The pus runs down my cheek
I love to pop and pop my zits
But no matter how many zits I pop
I get more again next week

"Pretty good, huh?" Finkelstein took a bite of his hot dog.

"Finkelstein, if this school gives you credit for that poem, I am officially dropping out."

"He-hurrggh, he-hurrggh."

"And will you stop with that laugh?"

"Okay," Alfred said. There was a pause.

"He-hurrggh, he-hurrggh."

I glared.

"Sorry, it's just how I laugh." He took a second bite of his weenie, then jammed two Tater Tots into his face. "What you gonna do your poem on?"

"Morons," I said.

"Niiice," he replied, as if I was really onto something.

I watched Finkelstein take a third bite of his hot dog and chew. He must have gone to the orthodontist yesterday. This week's color: cat-whiz frog vomit.

I would have been more disgusted by Finkelstein's Frankenstein teeth except I knew that in a few minutes, the bell was going to ring. And that meant it would be time for me to go face the dragon. The monster. The worst of the worst of all of possible nightmares.

Math class. It was time for my return.

My stomach fluttered. My shoulders got tense. I looked at my food. There was no way I could eat.

"He-hurrggh, he-hurrggh."

I looked up. Alfred was practically in hysterics.

"What're you laughing at, Finkelstein?"

"Morons," he answered. "You said morons."

"That was like ten minutes ago."

"I know," he replied. "But you were talking about me, right? That's funny. I'm glad we're best friends."

"Shut up, Finkelstein."

Bing-bong. Bing-bong. The bell rang. It was time to meet my doom.

I threw away my uneaten food and then began the long, slow march down the crowded school hallway.

Thwap! I got hit by another spitball. I pulled it off my neck and realized that this one seemed to have been dunked in chocolate milk. I didn't even turn around to see where it had come from.

Next stop . . . the executioner's chamber.

6

On my way to math class, three guys socked me, two tried to trip me and one tried to stick a Magic Marker so far into my ear that I thought they were going to color my brain. Maybe decontaminating Gramps's yellow belly-button ooze would've been a better way to go.

Also, I was concerned that I'd only had one boner all day, the one I woke up with. I swear those things were like roosters . . . up at dawn every morning, making it almost impossible to take a pee.

"Please," I said to the Gods of Stiffness. "Please don't torture me next period."

I didn't get a reply. Figures.

"Well, how am I supposed to manage these things, then?" I asked the Lords of Peckerdom.

Again, no response. *Urgh.* So frustrating.

In some ways, walking into math class felt like returning to the scene of a crime I never meant to commit. Of course, I sat down at my usual desk and tried to act as if everything was cool. As kids filed into the room, almost all of them had a comment, a look or a giggle for me. My life had turned into a source of nonstop chuckles for every student in the school. It was absolutely terrible.

And then it got worse.

While waiting for the teacher, I suddenly saw the girl who had said hi to me earlier in the day when Mom first dropped me off. Wow, she was the most beautiful girl I'd ever seen.

I stared as she crossed the room, taking in every small detail about her. The way the red and white stripes of her socks perfectly matched the red and white stripes of her shirtsleeve. That she had six bracelets on her left wrist but only two on her right. That she wore a silver thumb ring.

We made eye contact. I smiled. She smiled back.

Look at those green eyes. Amazing!

Now, I'm not one of those goofballs who believes in love at first sight—or in this case, love at second sight—or any nonsense like that, but when I saw this girl, something hit me.

Hit me hard.

And there was only one thing in the world I was hoping for just then.

That she'd been hit, too.

I stared at my mystery girl as she took a seat, one row up and one row over from me, the absolute perfect placement in class for me to gawk all day at this angel from heaven above.

I turned to Finkelstein "Who's that?".

"Her name's Allison Summers, and she's hot like barbecue corn," Finkelstein answered. "A new fishie in the pond, only her second day."

"She's beautiful," I said.

"Too bad for you she's also the new math teacher's daughter."

Suddenly, a shadow rose from behind me, darkening my desk. It appeared like a storm cloud.

"So, you're the famous Bobby Connor?"

Gulp. I slumped in my chair.

"My name is Mr. Summers, and I am the new mathematics instructor," he began. Mrs. Mank, it turned out, broke her hip, ankle and fibula during the tumble she took two days ago. Word was she'd be out at least six months, maybe eight.

"Now, I do hope there will be no more 'issues' for you in this classroom, Bobby," Mr. Summers said in a stern, serious voice. He had brown eyes, a strong jaw and the most perfectly groomed mustache I'd ever seen on a man. Black and straight and totally even. It was as if he'd measured every whisker with a ruler.

"Um, no sir," I answered. "No issues at all."

Of course, we both knew I was lying. The truth is that the compass in my corduroys could point due north at any moment, and there wasn't a dang thing to be done about it.

"Good," Mr. Summers said. From my upward-looking angle, I could see straight into his nostrils. They were like little pink caves with short, manicured hair. *Ew!* "Because I like order, Bobby," he continued. "Order is the natural state of the universe. Math has order. Productive citizens have order. Good students have order. But chaos-causers . . ." He paused, letting the words dangle in the air. "They upset order. And thus, they upset me. Are we clear?"

Call it a hunch, but for some reason I didn't feel as if I was Mr. Summers's favorite student at his new school. I mean, we'd only known each other for like eight seconds, but still, something told me that he already didn't like me very much.

Perhaps my reputation as a kid with a winkie that sends teachers to the hospital had something to do with it?

"I said, are we clear, Bobby?" he repeated.

"Yes sir," I said. "Very."

"Good." Mr. Summers turned and then called out to the rest of the class, "Students, take out a pencil."

Kids slowly began reaching into their bags.

"Now!" he barked.

The whole room jumped, then sprang into action.

"We're having a test on the materials I went over yesterday and you'd better do well. None of this 'learn it yesterday, forget it today' stuff, understand? You will have twenty minutes to complete the following twenty problems. Make sure you copy the question on your own sheet of paper. Do not write on my test." He began handing out tests to every student in the room. "And yes, you *must* show your work."

"But the bell hasn't even rung yet," Nathan said, finding it unfair to start class before class had even started.

Mr. Summers crossed his arms, squinted at Nathan and waited. His mustache waited, too.

Three, two, one . . .

Bing-bong. Bing-bong.

"I'll be expecting excellence, Nathan," Mr. Summers said. "Orderly excellence."

Nathan, without a peep, looked down and began his test. Obviously, there was a new sheriff in town.

Sheriff Mustache.

"Um, Mr. Summers," I said, meekly raising my hand.

"Yes, Bobby?" he answered impatiently.

"I wasn't here yesterday." I handed him back the test he'd just given me.

Sheriff Mustache looked at the piece of paper I was holding, but didn't take it. I spent eleven seconds holding out the set of math problems like a complete idiot.

"So . . . ?" he finally said.

I put the paper back down on my desk, clearly getting the message: Sheriff Mustache didn't care whether I had been absent or not. I still had to take the test.

I looked at question number one.

"Be sure to show your work, Bobby," Sheriff Mustache said before weaving his way up the aisle to look over people's shoulders whether they wanted him to or not. "No work, no credit."

I already hated this man.

Just then the angel turned around from one row up and one row over to mouth something to me.

"*Llrrffpth rrnnpf ffee,*" she said.

I shook my head, not understanding.

"Huh?" I mouthed back.

"*Llrrffpth rrnnpf ffee,*" she repeated.

I shrugged. "Huh?"

She paused to make sure no one was watching her. "It's eee-zee," she whispered.

"Allison!" snapped a voice from the front of the room.

The angel smiled at me with big red apple cheeks and then spun back around, not daring to turn around again.

Right then, I knew I was cooked.

Devastated.

Destroyed!

People called me Bobby Banana. People called me the Puny Pecker Pirate. People called me Mini-Man Connor Man, the Undersized Wiener Dog. All day long people called me the craziest names they could think of, and there was no telling when, or even if, it was ever going to stop.

But right at that moment, as I stared at a math question I had no idea how to solve, I suddenly realized I had a much bigger problem than spending the rest of my life as a sad, pathetic victim of stupid, immature erection jokes.

I was cuckoo in love with the new math teacher's daughter.

And she had a father named Sheriff Mustache who was ready to flunk me all the way back to second grade.

7

The room was dark and quiet. Clean. The air-conditioning was cold.

"Boys have a penis. Girls have a vagina." That was the first thing my correctional erectional therapist said to me. No name. No introduction. No warm-up. Just headfirst into a conversation about human privates.

I replied with supreme intelligence.

"Um . . ."

She was a woman with the body of a pencil. Skinny arms, skinny fingers, skinny neck. She even wore skinny glasses.

"Girls also have breasts," she continued. "Sometimes they cause arousal in men. Do you understand the word *arousal*, Bobby?"

"Um . . ."

"See, when your brain finds something to be arousing, it sends specific messages to your penis. Are you familiar with how the human penis accomplishes its biological functions, Bobby?"

"Um . . ."

"Think of your penis as something that has ears."

"Ears?" I said. "My penis has ears?"

"Yes, your penis has ears," she answered. "And when the ears of your penis hear sounds they find pleasant, the blood flow to your penis is temporarily increased and trapped in the penis so that your penis becomes elevated and enlarged. The scientific term for this process is called vasocongestion. Can you say vasocongestion?"

"Um . . ."

"Go ahead. Va-so-con-ges-tion."

"Vahz-oh-con-jest-chee-un."

"Good. Now let's look at some penile charts. Of the four penises that you see, can you identify which of the following penises are flaccid?"

A screen came down on the wall behind her, and suddenly there was a slide show.

Aarrgh! I jumped back in my seat. The detailed biological images in front of me freaked me out.

"The penis consists of three cylindrical masses, two corpora cavernosa and a third cord, the corpus spogiosum urethrae. The expanded distal end of the corpus cavernosum forms the glans, while this part extends to the urethra and is covered by a sheet of skeletal muscle, the bulb cavernosus."

I stared at the screen on the wall, frozen and terrified, having no clue what the heck this woman was talking about. Using a wooden pointer, my correctional erectional therapist explained the precise science behind a human erection. Truth is, right at that moment, I believed that correctional erectional therapy was gonna work perfectly, because after ten minutes with this skinny lady explaining all of this horrible information, I doubted I would ever have another boner in my life again.

"Here," she continued, "let me show you what it looks like from a different point of view."

She changed the slide.

AARRGH!

"Don't worry," she said with a laugh. "It won't bite."

I'd never seen such a twisted-looking hoffenschlonger. I think it was an inside-out point of view.

Blood rushed to my head. I felt dizzy. "Can I be excused?"

"Now, Bobby," she answered, adjusting her thin eyeglasses. "If you want to get better, you are going to have to make an effort. I can't do all the work myself. Puberty is a challenging time, and knowing the science behind your body is the first step toward helping your mind grow more comfortable with who you are. Please, work with me. We still have forty-three more minutes."

"But—"

"And you know, Mr. Hildge is expecting a report on this," she interrupted.

"A report?" I said.

"A full report," she answered. People with arms as thin as hers should always wear long sleeves, not sleeveless tops like the one she had on.

I decided to stop protesting. She switched slides.

Eeeeee!

For the next forty-three minutes I was given large quantities of penile information. Information about crowns, shafts, testes . . . There should be a law against those kinds of words. Then, when my session was finally over, she handed me a business card and explained our meeting schedule.

"We'll see each other every Tuesday and Thursday immediately after school for the next eight weeks and . . ." She stopped speaking. "What?" she asked.

"Ms. Cox?" I said, looking at the business card.

"Dr. Cox," she answered.

"Is that, um, what I call you?" I asked.

"Yessss," she said, stretching out the word. "It's my name, Bobby. Why, is there a problem?"

She glared at me over the rim of her skinny glasses.

"A problem? Um, no. No problem, Dr. Cox."

Hey, maybe I'll get lucky and her associate, Dr. Dick, will pop in for an office visit, too!

"As I was saying," she continued. "We'll meet twice a week, on Tuesdays and Thursdays immediately after school."

"Yes, Ms. Cox."

"Dr. Cox."

"Oh yeah, sorry."

She stared at me, daring me to make fun of her name. I didn't have the guts. But me and this Dr. Cox woman talking twice a week about peckers, I mean, wasn't there a better way?

"We're done for the day, Bobby," she said. "You may leave."

I wasted no time getting out of that office and stumbled home.

Walking down the street, a squirrel crossed my path. A moment later I had a pipe in my pants. Why the sight of a fluffy rat would make my pecker get stiff was something I'd never understand. But whatever. At least I was alone when it happened.

Perhaps if I concentrated on something else, my erection would go away? I thought about purple monkeys dancing with green parrots.

Nope, still stiff. Hmm . . . what to do, what to do?

I reached down my jeans, adjusted my equipment and continued toward home. At least boners didn't make you walk any different. They were like farts in that way. You could just cruise down the street without breaking stride and no one would ever know that you had just practically crapped your pants.

A few minutes later, I was at my front door. A front door that stuck ever since my dad had painted it green.

Ah, green, I thought, *the color of Allison's eyes.* My plan was to daydream the rest of the afternoon away, maybe eat a few chips and play a few video games to erase the torture of the psycho psychologist from my mind. But then there was a knock. I shouldn't have answered.

"So, did your therapist straighten out your boner? *He-hurrggh, he-hurrggh.*"

"Go away, Finkelstein."

Finkelstein had brown hair in a bowl cut, a few randomly splattered freckles across his cheeks and big ears. A person couldn't make a bigger dork if they had a middle-school-doofus-making machine.

"Aw, just messin', bro," he said.

Finkelstein was not only my classmate, he was my neighbor two doors down, my Little League teammate ever since T-ball and the son of my mother's favorite car-pool partner. We were even born in the same hospital the same week, delivered by the same doctor. The only time I am without Finkelstein in my life for long stretches of time is when he goes away to summer camp in North Carolina for six weeks every year.

Except last summer he came home early due to bee stings. For some reason, Finkelstein wanted fresh honey. It was a twelve-year-old boy in shorts and a tank top versus forty thousand angry honeybees in the middle of a hot summer day. They even stung his armpits. Alfred ended up having to be medevaced out of camp and was wrapped in special ointment gauze like some kind of mummy boy for three weeks. To this day, he does all he can to avoid even the thought of bees. It gives him flashbacks and stuff.

"Ya know, Bobby, the secret to erection management is duct tape," Finkelstein said, pulling out a roll of thick, silver tape. "I brought you some."

Duct tape? For a second, I actually thought about wrapping up my willie good and tight so that it wouldn't give me any more "pop up out of nowhere" problems. But just for a second.

"Leave, Finkelstein."

"Yeah, leave, zit face," Hill said, appearing from the kitchen with a glass of cranberry juice. Though my sister was only four foot eleven and eighty-seven pounds, ever since this school year started she had the attitude of a grumpy rhinoceros.

"I'll leave once you grow boobs, Hill. Oh, wait, guess that means I'll be staying another twenty-six centuries. *He-hurrggh, he-hurrggh.*"

"Metal mouth," she responded.

"Flat chest," he answered.

"Acne face!"

"Pipe cleaner!!"

"Will you two shut up?!" I shouted. Hill stuck out her tongue at Finkelstein. To show how mature he was, Finkelstein returned the tongue gesture and then he jammed a finger in his nose, another finger in his ear and stood on one foot doing some crazy hula dance like a pinheaded moron with a hamster in his underwear.

Hill shook her head and walked out of the room.

"Yeah, well, I gotta go finish anyway," Finkelstein said as he took his finger out of his nose and picked up a folder he had set down on the table. "Yep, just gotta go finish hanging up these flyers."

I ignored him.

"Aren't you gonna ask what flyers, Bobby?"

"No."

"Go ahead, ask."

"No," I repeated.

"Bet you will," he said.

"Bet I won't," I answered.

"Bet you will."

"Bet I won't."

"They're about you," he said.

"Whaddya mean, they're about me?" I shot back. "What are they?"

"See, I told ya you were gonna ask. *He-hurrggh, he-hurrggh.*"

"Shut up, Finkelstein!" I said, snatching the folder from his hands. I looked down and read the flyer.

Come celebrate
the First Annual Bobby Connor
BONE-A-THON

Have you ever had a woody in class?
Have you ever had to pretend you didn't have a raging stiffy?
Have you ever felt down because your pecker was up?
Don't let them oppress you anymore—stand up for your
right to allow your weenie to stand up.

Join us at the First Annual Bobby Connor
BONE-A-THON

This Friday, after school.
Don't be hard on yourself for being hard—
join your Boner Brothers.
It'll Be A Whacking Good Time!

"Um, Finkelstein . . ."

"Yeah."

"How many of these did you hang up?"

He paused. "Not many."

"How many?" I asked.

"Ten or so." He paused again. "Okay," he confessed. "Two hundred and sixteen."

"Finkelstein!!"

"What? All guys get erections," he said. "This'll be a show of solidarity. Fat Matt already said he'd DJ the event and his belly is so big, he's probably never even seen his pecker. This could be major!"

I quickly put on my shoes. "Let's go."

"Where are we going?"

"We gotta take 'em down!"

"All of them?" Finkelstein asked.

"Yes, all of them."

"And the website, too?"

"Finkelstein!!"

I grabbed him by his collar and we dashed out the door. There was no time to waste.

8

"There, all done," I said once we finally had the last of them.

"Wellllll . . . ," Finkelstein said.

"Well, what?" I said as I crumpled up the flyer. Why Finkelstein was posting boner flyers on the bulletin board of our local church was beyond me. I mean God'll throw a lightning bolt at you for that kind of stuff.

"Wellll . . . there's still one left," he said.

"Where?" I asked. "We'll go get it."

"Wellll . . . that might be tough."

"Why?"

"Wellll . . ."

I grabbed Finkelstein by the ear.

"Talk, Finkelstein!"

All the green grass around the church made me think that perhaps this place had a cemetery in the

56

back where I could just go murdalize and bury Finkel-stein right then and there.

"It's the original. *Ouch*," he answered. "Don't twist! I forgot about the original."

"So, where is it?" I demanded. "Give it to me."

"*Ouch*, I can't," he squealed. "Stop!"

"What do you mean, you can't?" I let him go.

"That really hurt, Bobby," he complained. "You know I have a sprained ear from the time I got my head stuck in the bars at the zoo."

"Finkelstein!" I was ready to rip his face off. "Where is the original?"

"I left it in the copy machine." He paused. "The copy machine at school."

Finkelstein covered his ears with both hands wait-ing for me to shred him.

"Let me get this straight. You left the original copy of the First Annual Bobby Connor Bone-a-Thon flyer in the school photocopy machine?" I said. "You're not serious?"

"Uh-huh." He nodded. "I snuck into the faculty lounge when no one was looking."

"Finkelstein!!"

"What?" he said. "I was just trying to help."

"We gotta get it."

"Impossible," he answered. "It's like a fortress in there. I was lucky to break in the first time."

"Finkelstein," I said. "You better figure out a way to get lucky again or else I am going to tear off your ear and staple it to your nose so you can smell your own pain."

"*He-hurrggh, he-hurrggh,*" he laughed. "You heard that on the wrestling channel."

"Shut up, Finkelstein!" I said. "And figure out a way for us to get back that original."

I dropped my head just thinking about it.

"Oh, what's the point?" I said, ready to give up. "I bet somebody already found it."

"Doubt it," said Finkelstein. "I did it after school and most of the cars were already gone from the teachers' parking lot."

"You think there's a chance it's still there?"

"Most definitely," he said.

Finkelstein rubbed his chin. "Okay, I got a plan," he said with sudden enthusiasm. "We'll wear black. All black. That way we can be inconspicuous."

The next morning Finkelstein and I set our alarms to get up at four forty-five so we could be at school by five twenty a.m. It was so dark, even the roosters were still asleep. But campus, we knew, would be open. That's because teachers are freaks, and a few of them were always around preparing new ways to torture students, even at five thirty a.m.

"Why aren't you wearing black?" I asked when I met Finkelstein on his front lawn.

"I was out of black," he answered. "So then I went for green, but it didn't match with brown, so I decided purple would be good, but it didn't match with red, so—"

"You're wearing bright yellow!"

He looked down as if he was seeing himself for the first time that morning.

"Not so inconspicuous, huh?"

"You look like a friggin' bumblebee," I exclaimed.

Uh-oh. Wrong thing to say. Finkelstein's face slowly began to turn white. I had just mentioned the word no one was ever supposed to ever say around him again: *bee.*

"Finkelstein? Finkelstein? Snap out of it! Oh, come on, Alfred, don't do this to me."

"Bzz, bzz," he muttered. Finkelstein started having a flashback.

I grabbed him by the arm and pulled him along. I didn't have time for this.

Sure enough, when we arrived, the front gate had already been unlocked. We went inside. Me, dressed like a ninja warrior, black on black. Finkelstein dressed like a flashing neon warning sign that you could see in a rainstorm from a hundred miles away.

"*Bzz, bzz,*" he muttered again.

School halls are kind of spooky when there's no one around. The corridors are sorta cheerful during the middle of the day with all the banners and posters and trophy cases and tons of students, but when you walk through empty school halls outside of regular hours, it feels like a mass murderer is going to pop out at any moment, slice open the middle of your belly and then make a chunky, bloody milk shake out of your spleen.

"Finkelstein, you with me? Finkelstein?" I said.

He had a faraway look in his eyes.

"Bees go *bzz*. Toast with honey."

This kid was damaged goods. I would clearly be on my own when the mass-murdering milk shake maker appeared.

"Come on," I said, pulling him along.

I turned the corner and headed for the door that said FACULTY LOUNGE. I tried the handle.

Locked.

Crud! Finkelstein was right. There was no way I was getting in without a key. Suddenly, I heard footsteps approaching from down the hall.

"Finkelstein, come on. We gotta hide."

"Hello, little yellow and black friend. *Zzzpp, zzzpp.* Pretty colors. Nectar."

"Finkelstein, come on. We gotta go!"

"Can I sprinkle you on my morning Cheerios?"

I tried to pull Finkelstein away, but it was too late, there was nowhere to hide, we were busted. A moment later, Allison Summers appeared from around the corner.

Allison Summers?

"Hi," she said.

"Um, hi," I answered, very surprised.

"You're here kinda early, no?" she asked. "It's Bobby, right?"

"Um, no," I answered. "I mean yes. I mean well, you know, yes, my name is Bobby and no, it's not so early." *Come on, Bobby, get it together.* "See, some days I get up early to make sure all my schoolwork is done and see if I can help any of the teachers out around campus. Teachers are so dedicated, you know? They really are America's heroes."

"Uh, yeah," she said with a sideways look. It was quiet for a moment. My eye drifted to a purple poster on the wall that said PARTICIPATE IN SCIENCE FAIR.

Um, no, thanks, I thought.

"How 'bout you?" I said, trying to get some sort of conversation going. "It's Allison, right?" Like I really didn't know that the most beautiful girl in the history of middle school was named Allison.

"Right," she said.

"You always here so early?" I asked.

"So far," she replied. "I mean my dad just got the new job and he wants to, you know, make a good impression. That's why he's taking on all kinds of extra duties and stuff. To prove himself."

"Extra duties?" I said. "Like beyond torturing the students?"

"Well, there's that of course," she said with a smile.

She smiled! She smiled! She smiled at one of my jokes! My heart started pounding like there was an elephant in my chest.

"He just got roped into chaperoning the dance," Allison continued. "You going?"

"Bzzz."

Allison looked at Finkelstein. I had to keep her attention off of him.

"Um . . . going?" I said. "Going to what?"

I stepped in front of Finkelstein to cut off Allison's line of sight.

"Bzzz . . . bzzz."

"The Big Dance," she said, still looking puzzled by Finkelstein. "You know, for eighth graders?"

"Oh, I . . . well . . . I don't know. Are you?" I asked.

"*Bzzz, bzzz.* Tasty breakfast. *Bzzz, bzzz.*"

"Maybe. I mean, I'm so new around here that . . . Is he okay?" Allison suddenly asked, wrinkling her nose.

"*Bzzz. Bzzz.* Cereal topping. *Bzzz. Bzzz.* Not a big hive. *Bzzz. Bzzz.*"

"Oh yeah, sure," I said. "He's fine."

But Finkelstein was not fine. Matter of fact, Finkelstein was cracking up. His voice grew louder and louder as his flashback intensified.

"*Bzzz, bzzz.* Soft fur. *Bzzz, bzzz.* Hold on, Mr. Bumbler. *Bzzz, bzzz, bzzz.* Wait, don't call your friends! *Bzzz, bzzz, bzzz.*" Finkelstein suddenly started screaming and swatting at imaginary bees in the air. "No need for reinforcements!! *Bzzz, bzzz. Bzzz, bzzz, bzzz.*"

Both Allison and I stared, not knowing what was going to happen next.

"*Aaarrgghh!!*" he screamed.

Finkelstein then began freaking out like he was being attacked by a swarm of honeybees.

"No need to hurt me. I'm just a little boy. *Ouch. Bzzz, bzzz.* Not my tushie!! *Ouch. Bzzz, bzzz!!*"

Suddenly, the door to the faculty lounge flew open and out came Nathan Ox.

Nathan Ox? What was he doing in the faculty lounge? His parents must have forced him to take advantage of that stupid extra tutoring the school had just started offering in the early mornings.

"What's all the noise?" Nathan demanded. "What is this goober freaking out about?"

"He thinks he's being attacked by imaginary honeybees," I answered.

"Imaginary honeybees? What kind of dork faces are the two of you? Make him stop, boner breath."

Nathan then knocked me in the balls.

"Ouch," I said. "I can't make him stop."

"All right, then I'll do it," Nathan answered.

Ya know, I never realized you could actually lift a person off of the ground by their nipples. Really, I would have thought they'd pluck off or something. But nope, turns out nipples are stuck on there pretty good.

Finkelstein's eyes began watering from the pain of being lifted into the air by his chest. It was the gnarliest titty-twister I'd ever seen.

However, it worked.

"OW! You're pulling off my breasts!" Finkelstein shouted as he woke from his daze. *"Let go!!"*

Finkelstein's scream echoed down the white halls. Nathan, always looking for a new way to torment somebody, gave one more turn of the dial for good measure and then dropped Finkelstein to the ground. Finkelstein collapsed with a thud that echoed, too.

"That was unnecessary," Allison said.

"It worked, didn't it?" Nathan laughed. "Back to idiot normal."

Then Nathan punched me in the garbanzo beans once more. This time, he knocked me so good my marbles clanked.

"Oy!" I yelped.

I bent over at the waist, turning blue as my coconuts rose up into my throat. A moment later, the door to the faculty lounge flew open again.

"What in the world is going on out here? Allison, what are you doing?" Mr. Summers, aka Sheriff Mustache, barked at his daughter.

She froze. I decided to be Prince Charming and come to her rescue.

"It wasn't her, sir," I answered, still bent over at the waist. "It was me. I, uh . . . I zipped my pants awkwardly."

Sheriff Mustache stared at me. His collar was stiff and his necktie was brown. I'd never seen such a crisp tie knot before.

"You know," I continued. "Like when you're tucking in your shirt and you accidentally zip yourself up too fast and the skin gets caught in the metal because you . . ."

I stopped speaking. Really, what was the point?

Sheriff Mustache looked at me like I was some kind of middle school moron. Then, just to make matters worse, he opened up a folder he was carrying and held out a sheet of paper.

I narrowed my eyes to read it.

Come celebrate
the First Annual Bobby Connor
BONE-A-THON

It was the flyer. He must have found it in the copy machine. Sheriff Mustache crumpled it up into an angry ball.

"You think I've never seen boys like you before, Bobby? Trust me, I've been around a long time."

"Come on, Alfred," I said, picking Finkelstein up off of the hallway floor. "Time to go."

The two of us slunk away, him rubbing his nips, me holding my walnuts, both of us in deep and serious pain.

Allison looked at me with pity. I left, not even bothering to say good-bye to my dream girl.

9

Later that afternoon, since it was Thursday, after the usual seventy-three boners I get per day without a clue in the world as to how to handle them, I walked into correctional erectional therapy to meet with Dr. Cox, feeling lower than low. I mean, here I was on the verge of actually talking with the bestest, nicest, most attractive girl I had ever known and all I managed to do was get punched in my corn kernels and make her father think I was dumber than a lamppost.

"Today we will try a different perspective," she said as I entered the room. Again she wore a sleeveless top. Her forearms looked like rulers. "No need to sit, Bobby, we're going for a ride."

"A ride?" I said. "Where?"

"Since the informational approach did not seem to make the inroads I had hoped, we are going to try the physiological approach to transformation through chakra alignment."

"Huh?"

"Yoga," she answered, tossing me some clothes. "We're going to yoga. You can change into those once we get to the studio."

Fifteen minutes later, I was standing in a wooden-floored exercise room with twenty babes-of-the-century.

And they were all wearing skintight leotards.

"I'm not too sure this is a good idea," I said as I looked around. A supermodel bent over at the waist two feet in front of me.

"Channel the energy, Bobby. Channel the energy," Dr. Cox instructed.

I paused.

"Um . . ."

A moment later, a second supermodel crossed the room and bent over, right next to her friend.

Uh-oh, I suddenly realized. They weren't friends. They were twins!

"No, really, Dr. Cox," I nervously said. "This is a bad idea."

Dr. Cox tied her sandy brown hair back into a ponytail and prepared for the start of class.

"Like, a bad, bad, bad idea," I continued pleading

with her. "Plus, these tight-fitting pants you're making me wear—"

"Channel the energy, Bobby," she instructed again.
Then Dr. Cox closed her eyes and took a long, slow,
deep, spiritual breath. "Just channel the energy."

10

"What kind of sick person gets kicked out of a yoga class!?" my father snapped. He was really mad that he had to leave work to come pick me up from the exercise studio. Seems he had planned to stay late to impress his boss. Kissin' up, that type of stuff.

"But it wasn't my fault," I answered as we walked through the front door.

Mom, of course, was already in a tizzy.

"Oh my goodness," she said as we entered. "I've mothered a pervert." Mom closed the front door behind us, hoping the Holstons wouldn't catch the drift of the latest news. "Talk to him, Phillip," she said to my dad as she spun the red oval charm of her necklace around and around and around on its gold chain. "Talk to him."

"I'm not talking to him," Dad said, taking off his coat. He loosened his tie but let it hang from his neck.

"You've got to talk to him, Phillip," Mom insisted. "Maybe he needs some kind of man-to-man chat?"

"He doesn't need a man-to-man chat," Gramps answered. "What he needs is a jar of Vaseline and a stack of dirty magazines."

Gramps, sitting at the dining room table, popped a yellow jelly bean in his mouth and smiled. Mom glared at him, then turned back to Dad.

"Phillip, you're his father, for goodness' sake," Mom said.

"So? He's *my* father," Dad said, pointing at Gramps.

"At least that's what his mother says," Gramps answered. "Me, I've never been too sure."

"Again with the epileptic milkman theory, huh, Pop?"

"All I have to say is two words: *sloped forehead.* Hillary, look closely," Gramps said to my sister. "Do I have a sloped forehead?"

"Oh my gawd, Grampa Ralph." Hill turned away violently. "Your breath smells like a goat."

"That's 'cause of the new milk I'm drinking," he answered. "Helps with flatulence."

"What's flatulence?" Hill asked as she buried her nose inside her shirt. She looked like she was about to vomit.

"You know, gas. Farts. The blow of the big brown butt trumpet," Gramps replied. "They say goat's milk makes your wind smell sweet like berries. Hold on . . ."

Gramps closed one eye, strained, then let one fly. It was a loud, rumbling, sounds-like-he-wet-his-underwear type of blast.

"Now tell me that doesn't smell like a boysenberry bush," Gramps said.

"Phillip, please talk to him," Mom said.

"Pop, don't fart in front of the kids." My dad shook his head.

"Not him—*him*!" Mom shouted. "Talk to Bobby. About being a pervert."

"I'm not a pervert," I said.

"Oh yeah?" Dad said as he took a seat in the living room. "Well, there's twenty-two angry yogis down at the gym who say otherwise, Mr. Stretchy Pants."

"It was a leotard," I answered. He looked at me funny. "You know, a leotard, like dancers wear."

"Are you gay?" my father asked.

"I'm not gay," I answered. "The stupid therapist made me wear it."

I would have thought that Dad might have remembered what it was like to be my age and suffer from stiffy-itis all the time, but apparently not.

"Why does there have to be something wrong with being gay?" Hill suddenly asked, offended. "Maybe I'm gay," she said, crossing her arms.

"You're not gay," he answered.

"How do you know? Maybe I am. And why does there have to be something wrong with it?" Hill asked. "You're a bigot, you know that?"

"Bigot schmigot," Dad said. "You're still not gay."

"Gay, gay, gay," Hill answered. "Gay, gay, gay!"

"Ssshhh, the Holstons," Mom said.

"Maybe Bobby's got that recessive gene that your mom's brother Frank has," Gramps offered. Just then I noticed that Gramps was wearing the same blue pajama pants he was wearing the day before. And the day before that and the day before that.

"We have an Uncle Frank?" I asked.

"Well, used to be Uncle Frank," Gramps said, clearing up the matter. "You probably know him now as Aunt Fran."

"Aunt Fran used to be Uncle Frank?" I said, looking at my mom in shock.

"Ssshhh," Mom answered. "Not so loud." She peeped outside at the Holstons' house, then closed the window blinds. "And be nice," she added after another turn of the charm on her chain. "You're talking about my broth . . . I mean sister."

"If I run away, none of you are gonna come look for me, are you?" Hill threw up her arms. "I mean, seriously, you will respect my wishes to be a homeless teen living on the streets, right?"

"Philll-iipp," Mom said.

"Don't worry, she's not running away," Dad answered.

"I'm not talking about that child," Mom said. "I'm talking about that one," she said, pointing at me.

"Nobody ever listens to me," Hill said. "Nobody ever takes my feelings into consideration."

Dad threw an angry look at Hill. I could tell he'd had about enough of this whole conversation already.

"Gay," said Hill, recrossing her arms. "Gay, gay, gay."

"You watch it, young lady," Dad said, pointing his finger at my sister. "You just watch your bananas." Dad then turned to Mom. "Look, Ilene, I can either raise a boy or I can raise a man, but I can't raise both a boy and a man. Make your play."

A silence fell over the living room.

"What the hell does that even mean?" Gramps asked.

"Grandpa!" exclaimed my mother. "Don't use the H-word."

Gramps shrugged as if to say, "Why not?"

"My house, my rules," Mom added. "And if you are going to stay here as our guest while your wife is visiting her sister in New Mexico, all I ask is that you please respect my wishes, okay?"

"I thought Gram was on a cruise," I said.

"Oh, um . . . yeah," Mom said. "On a cruise visiting her sister."

"In New Mexico?" I said, trying to figure it out.

All the adults shared one of those looks. Something was fishy.

"Phillip," Mom said. "Would you talk to your son, please?"

"Look, Ilene, this is a man thing," Dad said. "And though you're not gonna like hearing it, the truth is, I think you need a penis to understand the situation."

Mom looked as if she were about to faint.

"Bobby knows what I'm talking about," Dad said. "Don't you, son?"

It was a moment before I answered.

"Can I be excused?"

"I don't know," Mom replied. "Can you?"

I shook my head. "May I be excused?"

Suddenly, I just felt, well . . . bummed out. I mean, I thought families were supposed to support you. Mine just made things worse. Like, did other kids feel this way about the people who lived in their house?

75

"I guess you may," my mom finally replied.

"Hey, Bobby," Gramps called to me.

"Yeah?"

"Don't forget the Vaseline." Gramps grinned, then farted. "Ahhh . . . boysenberry."

I headed to my room as Mom and Dad began a half hour fight with each other, my mom nagging my dad to "talk to me" and my dad responding with comments like, "Wives like you are why God invented alcohol and TV."

Life sucked.

11

"Ya know what we need, Bobby? Ya know what we really, really need?"

"Finkelstein, freeze," I said. "Hold it right there."

We stopped dead in the center of the school hall-way. It was Nutrition Break, a fifteen-minute time slot our school built into the day's schedule, since class started at seven thirty and no one got to eat lunch until eleven fifty. They thought we needed a short energy break in the mid-morning to eat apples and munch pears. Mostly, we just talked, chowed potato chips and punched one another.

I grabbed Finkelstein by his shoulders so I could get a good look at him.

"Smile."

"What?"

"Smile," I repeated.

He smiled.

"What kind of crazy color is that on your teeth this week?"

77

"It's called sunrise and carrots," he said proudly.

"Sunrise and carrots?" I said. "You look like you swallowed a safety vest."

"Yeah, sexy, huh?"

"No, it's not sexy, Finkelstein," I replied. "It's not sexy at all. It looks like they should use your face as a crosswalk warning."

"He-hurrggh, he-hurrggh."

"Do not laugh, Finkelstein. Please, do not laugh." I continued walking down the hall, past kids with stuffed backpacks, untied shoelaces and enough candy in their pockets to open up a convenience store. Even on a mellow day, the hallway was loud and rowdy, filled with kids' random screams. The only time it got orderly was when Vice Principal Hildge cruised past, yelling things like "No running in the halls!" into his bullhorn.

The guy probably slept with that bullhorn.

"I wanted something extra special for the ladies," Finkelstein explained to me. It had been about two weeks since "the incident," so the spitballs dunked in chocolate milk had mellowed a ton. "I mean, face it, Bobby, we need to score chicks for the Big Dance. Hey, watch this," he said, and before I knew it Finkelstein had dashed across the hall and approached

78

Susan Montgomery, a short girl who had blue eyes and brown hair tied in pigtails.

"Hey, Swooozie Q-zie," Finkelstein said, trying to sound as if he was some kind of middle school Casanova. "My tongue is like dynamite and your lips are the gas, so whaddya say you and me go to the Big Dance and slurp face till our hair explodes?"

Susan paused, shifted her books from one arm to the other, then fixed her eyes on Finkelstein like a laser beam.

"I'd rather lick pig vomit."

"*He-hurrggh,* you're witty," Finkelstein said, flashing a mouthful of glowing orange. "But seriously, whaddya say?"

"No, I am serious." Susan didn't have a hint of humor in her voice. "I would rather lick vomit from the belly of a dead pig than go to the Big Dance with you." She adjusted her books again. "Never talk to me again, Alfred. Even if I am about to step in front of a speeding bus, never talk to me again."

Susan walked away and disappeared into the flow of student traffic. Finkelstein stood there and watched her vanish.

"So you'll get back to me, right?" he called out.

Susan didn't even bother to turn around.

"She wants to taste my taste buds," Finkelstein said as he walked back over to me.

"Yeah," I answered. "I can see that."

One thing I had to hand to Finkelstein, though, was that he was completely unfazed by rejection. For me, even the idea of being shot down by a girl sent rivers of panic flowing through my blood. But Finkelstein was different. It was like he wore some kind of coat of not caring what other people thought about him. You could insult him, make fun of him, tease him and roast him and still, he'd just roll along continuing to do his own thing. We were totally opposite like that. Me, I was jelly on the inside when it came to people rejecting me. I liked to be liked.

I looked down the hall and suddenly freaked out. Quickly, I dashed around the corner.

"What's wrong?" Finkelstein said, following me.

I peeked down the hall from my hiding spot.

"What?" Finkelstein said.

"It's Allison," I answered. "Allison Summers." She was walking our way, speaking with two girls from the softball team.

"Why are you hiding?" Finkelstein said. "Go ask her."

"Go ask her what?" I replied.

"Go ask her to the Big Dance," Finkelstein said.

"I'm not gonna ask her that."

"Why not?" Finkelstein said. "A tasty little frog leg like her isn't gonna last in the pond forever."

"You're a moron." I checked to see if she was still heading my way.

She was. Two seventh graders suddenly raced by, one kid chasing the other, trying to smash him. Kids always got really nutty during Nutrition Break. To a kid my age, fifteen minutes felt like a hundred hours, and there was a heck of a lot of trouble you could cause in a pretty short amount of time.

"But why?" Finkelstein asked. "Why not ask her?"

"'Cause I'm not."

"But why?"

"Because," I said, tracking her every move. "I'm not."

"Because why?"

"Because what if she . . ." I paused mid-sentence. "What if she says no?"

Finkelstein looked at me in disbelief.

"That's what you're afraid of?" he said. "Her saying no? Um, hello, news flash. Girls say no to me all the time."

"Can you blame them?" I said.

"You're missing the point, Bobby," he explained. "See, you gotta start thinking about all the spit-swapping you'll be able to do if she says yes. That's what keeps me so motivated."

"That's not why I wanna ask her," I said. "I mean, of course I want to kiss her, but, well . . . I wanna ask her because, you know, I kinda like her."

"You kinda like her?" Finkelstein said. "Like, you mean, as a person?"

"Yeah, is that so abnormal, you dipstick?"

Finkelstein looked at me like he was just figuring out something he'd never quite realized.

"What?" I said.

"You got it bad for this little blueberry pancake, don't you?"

"Shut up, Finkelstein."

"*He-hurrggh, he-hurrggh.* You gotta ask her, Bobby."

I leaned up close to the wall like one of those undercover cops in a detective show and peeked back around the corner.

"No way."

"Yes way."

"No way."

"*Yes* way."

Allison brushed a strand of hair behind her ears.

Jeez, just looking at this girl gave me the tingles. Weak stomach. Unsteady legs. Fuzzy brain. And I'd really never had the tingles before. Not like this. Just the sight of her made my cranium spin.

I gazed at Allison for a moment more.

"Ya think?" I said to Finkelstein. "Ya really think I should?"

"I know you should," he answered. "Trust me, chicks love it when you take firm control."

"And how do you know that?"

"Sunrise and carrots, bay-bee. Subconsciously, it's a color scheme that communicates power."

Finkelstein licked his thumb and then brushed back his eyebrows with spit.

"They're gonna lock you up one day. You know that, right, Finkelstein?" I said.

"*He-hurrggh, he-hurrggh.* Just go ask her."

"Really?"

"Go!" he said, pushing me into the hall.

"All right," I answered. "Don't push, don't push."

I stumbled up to Allison. Godzilla-size butterfly wings fluttered in my stomach. "Um . . . hi," I said.

Jennie and Pam, the two softball players she was talking with, left us alone to chat after a small giggle.

"See ya later," Allison said to them.

"Bye," they said in singsong reply.

Allison and I stood there for a moment in awkward silence, the buzz of kids goofing off and chatting in the halls all around us.

"Um, hi," I said.

"Hi," she answered.

There was a pause.

"Yeah . . . um, hi," I said again.

"You already said that," she replied. But she said it with a smile. Allison Summers had the kind of teeth dentists would use in Super Bowl commercials.

"I did?" Somebody lightly bumped me with their backpack and then walked on.

"Yes, you did."

"Oh, well, I just wanted to make sure you felt hello-ed enough," I told her.

"Hello-ed enough?"

"Um, yeah," I said. "Hello-ed enough."

"Explain."

"Explain?"

"Uh-huh." Allison shifted her books from one arm to the other. "Explain."

"Okay." I took a deep breath, not having any idea what I was about to say. "See, sometimes people don't really say hi all that well. They just kinda jump into conversation and start rambling and you can't hardly follow them at all. But a good *hi* at the start of the conversation prevents people from getting too far off track. That's why I wanted to make sure you felt hello-ed enough, to stay on track and not ramble and be a good hello-er."

Well, it was a good relationship while it lasted, I thought, but now that I had just proven to be the biggest putzwad she'd ever met, I guess it was back to the Land of I-Have-No-Idea-How-to-Talk-to-Girls for another few hundred years.

Allison wrinkled her nose. I wondered if Guinness World Records had a category for the shortest relationship in middle school history.

A teacher walking down the hallway checked his cell phone. A girl with curly hair and glasses took a drink from a water fountain. Time stood completely still.

"Oh," said Allison, unwrinkling her nose. "Then hi."

Was she hi-ing me back?

"Or should I say, hi-hi?" she added.

"Hi-hi?" I asked, unsure of where she was going with this.

"You know, so that people feel hello-ed enough," she told me. "Maybe we should just say hi-hi to each other instead of just hi, so that each of us feels hello-ed enough every time we see each other."

"Good idea," I said, my heart filling with hope. "I like it."

She smiled again, hitting me with a thousand watts of super-teeth. I melted like a marshmallow in a campfire.

"Hi-hi," she said, starting our conversation over from the top.

"Hi-hi," I replied, and I realized I was smiling, too.

Gulp. I was out of other things to say. It was like I had played my best card and miraculously it had worked. Now I was empty, totally and completely out of other stuff to talk about. Holy cow, I really didn't have any idea how to chat with a girl. How come school didn't offer classes on that?

Luckily, Allison picked up the slack.

"Were you going to ask me something?" she said.

"Um, yeah," I stammered.

The thing I don't like about some of the girls at my school is that so many of the good-looking ones were snobbish and pretty much more concerned with their hair than anything else. But even though I'd only known Allison for about two weeks, she seemed different. Sure, she painted her fingernails and wore a lot of cool bracelets, but she didn't wear gobs of makeup, and I never saw her staring into one of those pocket mirrors that the other girls were always looking into.

Especially when there's only two minutes left in

class. That's when you always see the pocket mirrors come out so that the bratty girls can make sure they look absolutely perfect in the halls.

Matter of fact, that's what gave me the idea last week to try the Pocket Mirror Test out on Allison.

See, Allison and I only had one class together, her dad's, so in order to run the Pocket Mirror Test, I had to find a spy. I chose Stephanie Teemer, a string-bean eighth grader who had really religious parents and a candy addiction. Sweets and sugary foods were all she ever ate, but her parents thought too many sweets were the path to the devil, so they made her give it up cold turkey. But since Stephanie had Allison in both her history and science class, and she was always on the lookout as to where she could score stuff like licorice and suckers and jelly beans, I thought I might be able to strike a deal to get the info I wanted.

Stephanie told me it would take six packs of Now and Laters, eight strawberry lollipops, two boxes of Hot Tamales and three packs of Mike and Ikes, plus a protractor, for her to do my dirty work.

I agreed, no problemo. Really, what did I care if she ate sugar nuggets for lunch? We met last Wednesday behind the basketball court.

"So what's she do when there's only two minutes left in class?" I asked Stephanie.

"You're not like a stalker, are you?" Stephanie was a full foot taller than I was.

I reached into the bag and held up a Giant Tootsie Roll, the kind that was as long as a table leg, and wiggled it in front of her face.

"Did I mention that I put a few little bonus treats into the bag?"

Stephanie looked down at the sack I was holding and licked her lips.

"Sometimes, she talks to a neighbor."

"Uh-huh."

"And a few times I saw her copy down the homework assignment from the board."

"Uh-huh," I said.

"And once she sneezed."

"Is that it?" I asked. "No pocket mirror?"

"Pocket mirror? What are you talking about? Now gimme the goods, a deal's a deal." Stephanie grabbed the bag from me. "And don't ask me to do this anymore. It's creepy."

"You sure there were no pocket mirrors?" I asked again.

"None," she said as she ripped open a bag of Sour Patch Kids and began to chug. "No pocket mirrors at all."

A minute later, her mouth was full of sugar. When

the sour taste hit her tongue, Stephanie's eyes rolled back into her head like an alien.

"Mmmm," she moaned.

That kid had issues, I thought. But my business with her was done. Allison had passed the Pocket Mirror Test.

Of course, I did the Pocket Mirror Test myself on Allison, but in math class. Her dad was the teacher, and since he was so strict, it made sense for her to behave. After all, if Sheriff Mustache couldn't control his own daughter, how was he ever gonna be able to control an entire room full of other people's kids?

Back in the school hallway, I looked into Allison's eyes. They were the prettiest green I'd ever seen.

"I was going to ask you . . . ," I said.

The inside of my stomach felt like there was a game of hopscotch being played in my belly.

"I was going to ask you . . ." The words about the Big Dance were just so close. "I was gonna to ask you . . . um . . . about your math homework."

"About my math homework?" she said, wrinkling her nose.

"Yeah, about your math homework. I just wanted to see if you, ya know, if you did it or maybe you needed any help with it or something?"

"Uh," she replied. "You do know that my father is the math teacher, right?"

"Oh, of course, of course." I tried to play it cool. "I just wanted to be sure that, you know, you felt like you had enough mathematical support just in case, you know, any mathematical challenges came your way. You know, mathematically, that is."

What the heck are you talking about, Bobby?

Suddenly, I felt a sharp elbow in the back.

"Hey, boner boy, knock, knock."

"Huh? What?" I turned around.

Oh no, I thought.

"I said knock, knock, weenie lips."

Nathan Ox pushed his giant chest right up against me. I swear that kid needed a bra. However, since Allison was standing right there, I figured I'd play along and try to act all cool.

"Okay," I said as if Nathan and I were old friends. "Um, who's there?" I turned to Allison. "Nathan is such a kidder."

She half smiled.

"Coco," Nathan blurted.

Call it a hunch, but something told me I didn't really want to hear the second part of this joke. "Um . . ." I tried to remain composed. "Coco who, Nathan?"

I smiled at Allison. *No worries, I got this.*

"Coco-NUTS!" he yelled, and then he punched me in my lima beans. I immediately folded over and turned blue.

"Have a nice trip to Planet Balls-in-Your-Throat, nut nose!" Nathan said with a laugh. Then he walked away.

Hunched over, I looked up at Allison and mustered up a grin.

"Yep, such a kidder." My voice was so high it sounded as if I had just sucked down a balloon full of helium. "See ya."

I shuffled away to go find a place where I could catch my breath. However, it was really tough to walk off in a cool-looking manner after my potatoes had just been mashed by the school butt-wipe.

Bing-bong. Nutrition Break was over. Just like my chance with Allison.

12

I walked into my house feeling smaller than a tadpole. A tadpole with a boner.

Jeez, these things were relentless. Up, down. Up, down. Up, down. What in the world was a guy supposed to do?

"Bobby, I've decided that you need more discipline," Dad said before I had even put my backpack down. Mom was nowhere to be found, and Dad was never the one home when I got back from school, so I knew something was up. "You can either wash the car or you can mow the lawn, but you cannot not wash the car and not mow the lawn. Make your play."

Mom had put him up to this, no doubt. I readjusted the stiffy in my pants in a way that made it look like I was just reaching into my pocket to feel for a set of keys or something.

After all, I knew all the hide-your-woody tricks.

"Whatever you want, Dad," I said.

Like I really care.

"Now trust me," my father said. "This is for your own good and you'll . . . Excuse me. What'd you say?"

"Doesn't matter." I tossed my stuff down. "I'll do whatever. You choose."

He studied me for a moment.

"What's wrong?"

"Nothin'."

"Hey, slugger," he said, softening. "Come on. What's up?"

He used to call me slugger all the time, back when we played baseball and did stuff together, but with him working so much and me developing a permanent case of erection-itis, well, he hadn't called me it in a long, long time.

And I can't say I missed it. Fact is, these days I sorta thought my dad was a goober.

However, I was desperate. But was I really desperate enough to seek help from my lame-o father?

"It's a girl," I said.

I guess I was.

"A girl?" he replied.

"Yeah, a girl."

He motioned toward the couch. "Come. Sit. Chat."

Suddenly, I regretted saying anything.

"C'mon, slugger," he repeated. "Sit down."

I let out a sigh and trudged over to the couch.

"You're not gonna give me a birds-and-bees talk, are you?" I asked. "'Cause that would be, like, awkward."

"Just sit down and tell me what's up."

Dad loosened his tie and kicked off his shoes. He wore tan socks that perfectly matched his tan shirt.

I told him all about Allison. About my feelings for her. About how I had the tingles for her and about how cool she was and about how green her eyes were. And also about how I really wanted to ask her to the Big Dance but chickened out and now felt just so miserable and stupid and loserly.

I let it all out. Dad didn't interrupt once. It must have been a record length of silence for him.

"I can help you," he said once I'd finished.

"You can?" I said.

"Yep, I can." He sounded so confident and sure. Maybe my dad wasn't such a goober after all?

"Okay."

"You see, Bobby, what you need to realize is that our family are second-place people. We're not the number ones in life. We do best when we play it safe. Take the conservative route. Don't stretch. If you don't expect too much in this world, you won't ever be too disappointed. The stuff of champions and victors, that's TV, that's not the Connor family."

I looked at him sideways. He leaned forward to make sure he was being clear.

"The problem you're having is that you're a second-class guy chasing a first-class girl. Fix your expectations and you'll fix the problem."

Huh?

"Stay within your limits, Bobby. Know who you are and you'll avoid a whole lot of troubles in this world, son. That's how I picked your mom, you know. No stretching. No reaching. No head all up in the stars," he said. "See, she and I are in the same category. We're both down here," he said, holding his hand a little lower than his waist. "Does that make sense?"

"Um, yeah," I stuttered.

"You sure?"

"Yeah, Dad. Um, thanks," I said, standing up.

"Don't mention it, Bobby. Remember, aim low. Play conservative. Grab the stuff that's easily within your reach and let the rest of the junk go," he said. "You get more of what you try for if you don't try for that much, if you know what I mean. It's a recipe for life that will take you far."

"Yeah, Dad," I said. "Thanks."

"Don't mention it, slugger."

Dad reclined in his chair. I could tell that he

felt good about just having had a real man-to-man talk with his son. It seemed like he felt—what's the word?—satisfied.

I went straight to my room, closed my door and opened up the school's e-link phone directory. A moment later I dialed up Allison on video chat.

Yep, Dad's words had set me straight. I knew exactly what I needed to do.

"Hey, Allison," I said when her face came on the computer screen.

It took a second for her to realize who I was.

"Don't you mean hi-hi?" she said with a thousand-watt smile once she saw it was me.

"Oh yeah, right," I said. "Hi-hi. Look," I began. "You know today when I saw you in the halls and asked about your math homework?"

"Uh-huh," she answered.

"Well, I don't care about your stupid math homework. What I really wanted to do was ask you to the Big Dance, but I chickened out because I didn't have the guts," I said. "But now I do have the guts, so I'm gonna tell you three things: One . . ." I took a deep breath. "I think you're beautiful. Two," I continued, not letting her get in a word edgewise, "I think you're a really nice, really cool person. And three," I added, not slowing down for anything, "you make me feel, I don't know, good on the inside when I see you in the halls or in class and stuff like that. I mean, it's like, I don't know, I just think you're special."

I paused.

Maybe I was making a fool of myself? Maybe I was creating yet another embarrassing, shameful, every-kid-in-the-school-is-going-to-hear-about-this-and-laugh-at-me moment? Maybe tomorrow the entire universe would have yet another reason to snort, giggle and hoot at Bobby Connor.

But so what? I didn't care. Screw my dad, I needed to reach. 'Cause if I didn't, I think a part of me would have died.

"Allison, I think you're amazing and I'm one hundred percent convinced that you need to attend the eighth grade dance with me, because I'm sure we'll have a great time together. And if you do not say yes right now, I am utterly certain it will be the greatest, most horrific tragedy in my young and absolutely pathetic life. So whaddya say?" I took one more deep breath. "Will you go to the Big Dance with me?"

Then there was silence.

13

"Hey, Bobby, wanna hear my new poem for English class?"

"I don't want to hear your new poem, Finkelstein."

"Bet you do."

"Bet I don't."

"Bet you do."

"Bet I don't."

"You know, Bobby," said Finkelstein. "It's really hard to be best friends with someone who is so emotionally withholding."

"We're not best friends, Finkelstein."

"See?" he answered. "Withholding."

We stood in the center of the crowded hall. A banner made of blue paper advertising the Big Dance in red and black Magic Marker writing had been taped to the wall.

Of course, I couldn't tell Finkelstein that Allison had agreed to go to the dance with me. It would simply break the poor kid's heart to discover I had a date and he didn't, but the fact is, I don't think God had yet invented the girl crazy enough to attend a school dance with Alfred Finkelstein. Sure, he pretended not to care about all the rejection, but deep down, I am sure he was sad about being turned down so many times. Knowing that, I decided to keep the fact that I had a Big Dance date a secret and listen to his poem, just so I didn't hurt his feelings.

"You know what, Finkelstein, I'm in a good mood today. Why not? Hit me with this English-class poem of yours. If it's good enough, maybe I'll steal it, because I haven't even given two seconds of thought to mine yet."

"He-hurrggh, he-hurrggh."

"What? Why are you laughing?"

"I knew you were going to want to hear it."

"Shut up, Finkelstein."

"Farts," he began.

The wind in my hair
The wind from my rear
Winds merging
Farts

The gas at an Exxon
The gas that I pass on
Gas you can count on
Farts

The stink of a cheese
The stink when my mom says, "Oh, Alfred,
     please"
They stink like a flower does for bees
Farts

He stopped. I guess that was the end.

"Finkelstein, you're the worst poet this planet has ever produced."

"*He-hurrggh, he-hurrggh*. Doesn't matter what you think," he said. "My goal is to score chicks."

"And you think you're going to score chicks with a fart poem?" I said.

"Beautiful words are beautiful words, Bobby, and chicks dig poetry," he answered. "I mean look at all the ugly guys that write lyrics and sing in bands. They score chicks like crazy. And why?"

"Because they're not you?" I said.

"Because of poetry, Bobby," he replied. "Chicks love poetry. Never forget that."

Suddenly, Finkelstein darted across the hall.

"Hey, Caroline, wanna hear some romantic words that'll make your heart melt and your top accidentally fall off?"

"Eat cow dump, brace face."

Before Finkelstein could even make another plea, Caroline Shea, a girl with only nine and a half fingers due to some kind of exercise bicycle accident when she was four years old, rushed away.

Finkelstein walked back over to me.

"She wants to taste my taste buds."

"I can see that," I said. We started walking toward PE, but since we still had twelve minutes left for Nutrition Break we were in no hurry. Finkelstein took out a package of cherry Pop-Tarts. Me, a bag of M&M's.

Peanut, of course.

"That poem is due next week, you know," he told me, taking a bite.

"I'll get to it," I said, tearing open the yellow M&M bag. "I'll get to it."

Suddenly, we heard a loud scream in the hall.

"YAAAAAYYYYYY! WAAA-HOOOOOO!"

It was Angie Rumpkin, a girl known for her big earrings, big bracelets and even bigger mouth.

"A Secret Someone! I got a Secret Someone!! *Yesssss*!" she screamed.

Angie dashed down the hall holding an invite to the Big Dance in her hand like it was some kind of winning lottery ticket.

"Aw, man," Finkelstein said. "Bobby, we gotta do something to score chicks for the Big Dance."

"How 'bout doing the Secret Someone thing?" I suggested.

"Naw," said Finkelstein. "That's cheating. I mean I wanna ask a girl to the dance and have her say yes to my face."

"What's the difference?" I asked.

"Because what happens if they say yes and then see that their Secret Someone is a total loser that they don't really want to go to the dance with in the first place? Then the whole thing gets weird, 'cause you're with someone who really doesn't want to be with you."

"Nobody wants to be with you, Finkelstein," I explained. "You do realize that, right?"

"You're so funny I forgot to laugh, Bobby," he said.

"I'm not being funny, Finkelstein," I answered. "I'm just making a scientifically provable point."

"Okay, let's be honest for a minute," he said. "I'm not the world's most handsome gentleman."

"Your face looks like a monkey's butt, Finkelstein."

"Can you try to stay focused with me here for a second, please?" he asked.

"Sorry," I said. "My apologies. Go on."

"And I admit, my standards are low," he continued. "I mean I'll take anyone to the Big Dance. I don't care if she's fat, smelly, pimply or cross-eyed. I really don't care."

"So then why not give a Secret Someone out?" I said.

"Because the chances to slurp face go way down if you go the mystery-invite route," he explained to me. I could tell he had spent a lot of time thinking about this whole thing. "But this way, if I ask someone and she says yes, secretly, we both know this means that in the middle of the dance floor I can expect to suck such deep face with her that she'll be able to identify what I had for breakfast."

"You really are Mr. Romance. I mean, I am just amazed that girls are not flocking to you."

"Nope," he replied as we made our way toward the gymnasium. "I'm gonna do it the old-fashioned way. No mystery envelope, Secret Someone, fooling a chick into going to the Big Dance with me. I'm gonna ask and ask and ask until I hear a yes. Hey, I'm seeing the orthodontist today, but let's get together after school tomorrow and map out a plan for the two of us."

"Can't," I said. "Have therapy."

"Aw, man, this is important," he answered. "Can't you get out of it?"

"I wish."

"That blows."

"Sure does."

Michelle Delphers approached from up the hall. She wore red sneakers with a double set of shoelaces, one pair red, and one pair white, on each of her feet. It was the latest style.

Finkelstein jumped in front of her.

"Hey, Michelle, wanna go to the Big Dance with me?"

"Oh, I'm sorry, Alfred," Michelle replied in a kindly tone. "I'm already going with Jeffrey Corbin."

"But you would have, right?" Finkelstein said in a hopeful way.

Michelle smiled warmly. "Not a chance," she answered. "No no way way ever, ever, ever."

Michelle started back down the hall.

"She didn't have to double up her words like that," I said to Finkelstein.

"She only did it because she wants to taste my taste buds," Finkelstein replied.

"Clearly," I said.

Finkelstein looked troubled. And he was starting

to get desperate. Girls hate desperate. It's like bad cologne.

Jimmy Morgan, the left fielder on my summer league baseball team, walked by and nodded to me, but then kept going. Clearly, I was still an outcast to all of my other so-called friends. None of them were ready to actually stop and be seen talking to me yet.

Except Finkelstein. That got me thinking.

"You know, you really oughtta consider a Secret Someone," I said, trying to help him out. "I mean, these things were invented for morons like you."

Finkelstein took another bite of his cherry Pop-Tart.

"Bobby," he said. "I ain't giving up. It only takes one *yes* before I'm tasting taste buds."

Just then, I saw Allison walking up the hall.

"Besides, I don't see any ladies flocking to you," Finkelstein added.

"Um, yeah, you're right. Look, Finkelstein," I said distractedly, "I gotta go."

"What?" said Finkelstein. "Where? What about PE?"

"I'll meet you there."

"But . . . *Oooh*," he said in a sly voice once he saw I was heading toward Allison. "Still working on putting a hunk of butter on that piece of cheese toast, are you?"

"What are you talking about, Finkelstein?"

"Chicks dig persistence. Good plan, Bobby," he said. "Me, I've been too easy to give up."

Finkelstein then ran up to the first girl he saw.

"Hey, Pauline, if you don't go to the Big Dance with me, I am gonna stalk you," he said. "So say yes now or say yes at two o'clock in the morning when I am in a tree outside your bedroom window singing out-of-key love songs."

Pauline dropped her books and got into a tae kwon do stance. "Stay clear, Alfred," she said. "I know martial arts because of people like you."

"Oh, what, are you gonna hit me?" he said.

"Don't touch me," she warned.

"You mean I can't even touch you like this?" Finkelstein extended his finger.

"Don't do it."

"You mean don't do this?" he said, moving his finger even closer.

"I'm warning you, Alfred," she said as his finger inched closer. "Do not make physical contact with me."

"You mean not even contact like this?" Finkelstein said with a smile on his face. His finger was less than a centimeter from her forearm.

"Alfred . . ."

And then he did it. He touched her.

First there was a yell. *"Hii-yaa!"*

Then there was a scream. *"Ouch!"*

Finkelstein raised his hands to his neck and struggled to speak. "You just . . . punched me in the throat."

"Kee-daahh!" Pauline said, firing again.

"Ouch! Stop!"

"This was on the green belt test," Pauline said. *"Hoy-ya!"* She attacked with a series of moves.

Finkelstein screamed like a girl. "I have tender collarbones. Ouch!"

Finkelstein, brave hero that he is, ran off. Pauline chased right behind him. Some girls, as Finkelstein was learning, you just don't mess with.

But other girls you do. You definitely do.

"Hi-hi," I said with a smile as Allison approached.

"Hi-hi," she answered. For the first time ever I didn't feel nervous or scared talking to a girl. Of course, I was super-excited, but also, I felt like, well . . . I just felt like I could kinda be myself.

I offered her some M&M's.

"Peanut?" she said, looking at the bag.

"Of course," I said, popping one in my mouth. "It's the only kind I eat."

She smiled and stretched out her hand. "Me too," she said. "Peanut or nothing."

I poured a few into her palm. "You walking home later?" I asked.

"Yeah," she said. "You?"

"Uh-huh," I answered. "Wanna maybe walk together?" I tossed a red M&M into my mouth. "I mean, usually my helicopter picks me up, but today, I guess I could make an exception."

"Oh, an exception, huh?" she said, eating a blue one.

I couldn't believe I had come up with such a smooth line.

"I like your ponytail," I told her.

"Thanks."

Oh my God, I've never operated like this around the ladies in my entire life. Suddenly, my sister approached.

"Mom said to tell you that your therapy appointment has been—"

"Okay," I said, cutting her off. "Got it. Thank you. See you at home."

Hill kept talking. And I kept trying to stop her.

"And that you need to—"

"O-kay," I interrupted, reaching over to cover her mouth. "Got the message, loud and clear."

She pushed my hand away.

"And that when you get to—"

"Got it," I said. "Got it, got it. *Muchas gracias.*"

108

"Stop, ya freak!" Hill snapped at me. "And quit touching me with your grubby hands. Who knows how many times they've been down your pants today." She wiped her mouth with her sleeve. "I hope you washed."

I looked at Allison and faked a laugh. "She's cute, isn't she?"

"Shut up, Bobby," Hill said. "Just shut up for a stupid minute 'cause I don't want to be here talking to you any more than you want to be talking to me, and Nutrition Break is almost over. But Mom told me to tell you that your pecker therapist changed your appointment."

"Okay, moving along now . . ."

"And don't give me attitude, either," she said. "I mean, I'm not the one who's got the entire neighborhood thinking that we're a family of perverts."

"Great to see ya. Appreciate the time . . ." I pushed her away.

"Take your hands off me, jerk. Your psycho appointment with the wacko doctor is now today instead of tomorrow. Mom said don't be late 'cause the therapist is still mad about you popping a boner in front of all those yoga freaks."

I stood there with nothing else to possibly say.

"Geesh!" said Hill. "You are such a zero."

She stormed away. A moment passed.

"That's my sister," I finally said to Allison.

"You have the same nose," she replied.

"She's in seventh grade," I added.

"I like her belt."

"She hates me," I told her.

Allison reached out, took my bag of M&M's, then popped a yellow one into her mouth.

"Really? I couldn't tell," she said, chewing.

"Seems I kinda gotta go somewhere after school," I said.

"Your helicopter?"

"The yacht," I said. "Just had it painted."

Allison turned the bag upside down and poured the last two M&M's into her hand.

"Got it," she said.

"But maybe we could walk together tomorrow?" I asked hopefully.

Allison crumpled up the empty bag. Of course, she was going to dump me, tell me she had changed her mind about walking home with me, changed her mind about being friends with me and, worst of all, changed her mind about going to the Big Dance with me.

After all, if I were her, that's what I would have done. Clearly I was mayor of a city called Loserville.

"Ya know, Bobby," she began.

"Yeah," I said, completely understanding.

"Walking with you tomorrow, well . . . ." She paused. "My limo driver, he's got this schedule to keep."

I raised my eyes. "Your limo driver?"

"What?" she said. "You think you're the only one with a private chauffeur in this neighborhood? Get with the program. This is middle school. If you don't have a limo driver, you don't have anything."

She popped a brown M&M into her mouth.

"Right," I said with a big smile. "Well then, check with your driver and let me know."

"I'll do that," she answered.

"You know how to contact me?" I asked.

"I do," she said.

"Are you sure?"

"Yes, Bobby, I'm sure. I do have a school e-chat account, remember?"

"Oh yeah," I said. "Well then, okay . . . um, bye-bye."

"Not bye-bye," she said. "One bye."

I cocked my head to the side, not quite understanding.

"Two hi's, one bye," she explained. "Hi-hi because it's good to see each other, but one bye because it's not as good to leave. And bring more M&M's tomorrow," she added. "My dad only lets me bring fruit."

Then she popped my last M&M, a green one, into her mouth and munched.

If it would have been legal to get married while still in eighth grade, I swear I wouldda headed out ring shopping right then and there.

She turned and waved. "Bye," she said.

"Bye."

The rest of that day I was unable to walk to any of my classes. All I could do was float. I was feeling sky-high, like nothing in this whole entire world could bring me down.

When I got to the brown door inside the counseling office after school, I gave three small knocks to a little musical beat that played in my head, then entered.

"Happy Wednesday, Dr. Cox."

"Happy Wednesday to you as well, Bobby," she answered. Today's sleeveless top was navy blue. I could see the veins running all the way up her biceps. "Sorry I had to change appointment times."

"No worries."

"Well, I'm glad you're in a good mood, because today we're going to take the Freudian approach."

"Whatever," I answered.

"Please, have a seat on the couch."

I lay back. *Hey,* I thought, *this thing's pretty comfortable.*

"All right, fire away." I was ready to take on the world.

"Okay, we'll begin with a few basic questions." Dr. Cox took out a notepad and adjusted her skinny eyeglasses. "Have you ever seen your mother naked?"

"What!?"

I shot up off the couch, but gently, she pushed me back down.

"It's okay, Bobby. A lot of boys your age are curious about the female body."

"My mom's not a female," I said. "She's, like, a mom."

"All right, tell me about your father. I assume you've seen him naked, correct?"

"Do we have to talk about this?"

"Tell me," she said, looking over the rim of her glasses. "Would you say the dimensions of your father's penis are, one: intimidatingly large; two: exceedingly small; or three: appropriately sized for a man of his height and weight?"

"Um . . ."

I did everything I could *not* to think about my dad's pickle.

"I'll read the options again. One: intimidatingly large; two: exceedingly small; or three: appropriately—"

"Can I use the restroom?"

"You need to pee?" she asked.

"I need to puke," I said.

She looked down at her little chart and checked off a box.

"Still reluctant to participate in his recovery," she said to herself, but loud enough for me to hear it. "Recommendation: extended analysis."

14

Now, everyone my age knows there is really only one place you are not allowed to get a boner. Nope, it's not church. I've sported wood on the pew a bunch of times. And no, it's not the swimming pool, either. Although I do admit, bathing-suit boners are the worst. Ain't no backstroke when you have one of those woodies going, I tell ya that. No, the only place you are not allowed to get a boner is in the boys' locker room. It's like an unspoken rule of life or something.

Of course, it's not really fair that they make all the boys get naked with one another at the same time. I mean, just because I'm in eighth grade doesn't mean that I'm as big as some of the other eighth graders.

Not that I'm a pecker peeker or anything.

See, when you're getting naked in a room full of other naked people, as I happened to be doing the next day, it's kind of like driving by a car accident. You don't want to look to see what the damage is, but you kind of can't help yourself either, and most of the time you do end up catching a glimpse. But to do that in the boys' locker room is strictly off-limits.

Me, I strip and I dress. No small talk. No extended towel drying. No allowing my wanker to flop around in front of other people. Strip and dress, that's the rule.

"Hey, Bobby, want to hear my latest poem for English class?"

Arrgh!

"Finkelstein!! Put on some clothes."

"What?" he said. "We're all men here."

I turned away from Finkelstein's hairless bologna. Jeez, the kid didn't even have a sprout of pubes yet?

"Finkelstein," I ordered. "Put on some clothes and stop staring me in the face with your dinglehoffer, ya freak."

"Okay, you don't want to hear my poem for English class, fine. Let's hear yours," he said, putting his hands on his hips.

"I haven't done it yet," I said, looking away. Still no towel.

"You know you can't pass English this quarter without having recited a poem in front of the class, Bobby," he informed me. "And if you don't pass third quarter English, they automatically make you go to summer school."

"I'll do it," I said.

"When?"

"I said, I'll . . ."

Just then, while trying to avoid looking at Finkelstein, I noticed Tommy Williams.

And he had the hugest schlong I had ever seen!

My God, it was the thickest, beefiest, longest, down-to-his-knee pecker I had ever witnessed on an eighth grader. And I bet that when he got a boner, it grew to be the size of a big-league baseball bat.

"Uh, Bobby . . . ?" Finkelstein asked.

I didn't respond. Tommy possessed the most mammoth tube ever attached to a thirteen-year-old boy in the history of children. Elephants had less reproductive material.

"Um, Bobby . . . ," Finkelstein said again.

How did Tommy even walk?

"Hey, Bobby, snap out of it! What are you doing, staring at Tommy's penis?"

Suddenly, every boy in the locker room froze . . . then turned to stare at me.

"Shut up, Finkelstein!" I said. Jeez, why don't you use a megaphone?

But it was too late.

Tommy quickly pulled up his underwear. I quickly pulled up mine. Python boy wore jungle-print boxers. Me, I wore tighty-whities.

So pathetic.

"Dude, you staring at my wang?"

"No, of course not. No way, man."

Oh God, I had just broken the golden rule of the boys' locker rooms: no pecker peeking.

Tommy stepped so close, we were nose to nose. Actually, we weren't nose to nose because he was six inches taller than me. I had to bend my head all the way back just to keep eye contact with him.

"I'm going to ask you just one more time, Connor: Were you staring at my dong?"

"Staring? No," I said, my heart beating about a million miles a minute. "I mean, did I accidentally take a look?" I continued. "I might have. You know, a little glance, like the kind when a person is searching to find the clock on the wall, but instead sees another boy's sexual organ."

Bam! Tommy punched me in the face. The force knocked me over a locker-room bench and I crashed to the gray tile floor.

"Fight! Fight! Fight!" Finkelstein shouted, cheering us on like we were gladiators.

Why is Finkelstein cheering? I thought. I mean, I had already taken one shot to the head and if I got up, Tommy would have pulverized me into hamburger.

I stayed down. Besides, I'd been pecker peeking; I kinda deserved to get popped.

Tommy glared. "Keep your eyes in your own head, punk!" he said, and then he stormed off.

A moment later, I picked myself up off the floor.

"Wow, Bobby, are you okay?"

"Shut up, Finkelstein."

I touched the side of my face, right below my eye.

"He really nailed you good."

"Would you shut up, Finkelstein?" I said.

Ow, that really hurt, I thought.

If only, however, that was the greatest pain I was to suffer.

15

My brain was hazy for the rest of that day after I'd gotten walloped by Tommy. All afternoon long I couldn't focus on a darn thing.

I couldn't pay attention to any of my teachers' blabbering.

I couldn't focus on stupid Nathan Ox as he called me a hundred thousand penis-themed insults.

I wasn't even able to pay attention to the three more times that Alfred Finkelstein said "She wants to taste my taste buds" when another round of girls rejected his invitation to the Big Dance.

All I could concentrate on was one thing. And it wasn't my eye. Okay, I'd been bopped. Big deal. Like I said, I deserved it. No, I was being distracted by something else entirely: walking Allison home from school. As each minute passed bringing us closer to the end of the day, I got more and more excited. And jumpy. And happy and nervous, too. Truly, the last bell to end the last class of that Thursday could not have come fast enough.

"Hi-hi," Allison said when she saw me walking up the hall. Funny how the entire afternoon I was rushing to get to this moment, but now that it had arrived, all I wanted to do was slow time down, like have each second on the clock take an hour or something.

It's weird how girls can make your head so fuzzy. More fuzzy than a punch, that's for sure.

"Hi-hi," I responded.

"What happened to your face?"

"Navy SEAL mission. Can't really talk about it," I said. "Sometimes I work for the government."

"Saving hostages?" she asked.

"Taking out terrorists, disabling nuclear devices," I answered. "All while doing math homework for your dad."

"Sounds like you're pretty busy."

"Not too busy to walk you home," I answered. "And look what I brought."

I took out a yellow bag of Peanut M&M's. She smiled.

"Of course, I don't know what *you're* gonna eat," I added.

She laughed. I tore open the bag and poured three or four into her hand.

Smooth, Bobby. Real smooth.

We headed toward the front gate of campus, over the grass no one was ever supposed to walk on—which kids always did—side by side. Even though there were like fifty million students all around us, it felt like Allison and I were the only two people on the planet.

"So, what's it like being a teacher's kid?" I asked.

"You get answers to all the tests."

"You do?" I said.

"Naw, I wish," she replied. "Basically, it's like being any other parent's kid, I guess. I mean, my dad still treats me like I'm three years old, I hit him up for money when I need stuff, and he's hopeless when it comes to new technology. He stills uses a calculator from, like, the nineteen eighties."

"I wasn't even born yet," I said.

"Google wasn't even born yet," she answered, popping a yellow M&M into her mouth. "Other than that, he drives me to school in the morning, but I walk home by myself because he usually stays late doing teacher things."

"Where's your mom?"

"She died."

"Oh," I said. "Sorry, I . . . I didn't know."

"That's okay. It was a long time ago." We crossed

the street. "I don't really remember her all that much. Just been me and my dad for most of my life."

I stepped over a piece of broken sidewalk. "Not having a mom, you miss that?" I asked.

"That's kinda personal, isn't it?"

"I, um, yeah . . . I just . . ."

"No, it's okay," she said, opening up. "I guess so . . ." I offered her another M&M but she waved me off. "I mean I guess I don't really miss it so much 'cause I never really had one, ya know?"

We took a couple of steps without speaking. The fact that she'd stopped eating the M&M's made me think I'd upset her.

"I guess I do miss having a mom, now that I think about it," she suddenly added. "Especially when I hear other kids complain about how their moms nag them about this and that. It makes me sometimes wish I had that, ya know?"

"Yeah, sure," I said. I guess I never really thought about the positive side of my mom giving me all the grief she did. But she was always such a pain in my butt that it was sorta hard to look at it that way.

"Of course, kids think they don't want that stuff, but deep down, they do. They all do," she said. "It let's 'em know they're loved."

"Wow," I said. "That's deep."

"Deep?"

"Yeah. I mean usually I just walk home with Alfred Finkelstein and all he talks about are boogers."

"Boogers?" she said, scrunching up her face.

"You wouldn't believe some of the things that come out of that kid's mouth," I said. "Or nose," I added with a laugh.

She didn't laugh back.

Watch it, Bobby, you bonehead. Don't gross her out. Think of something classy to say.

"But sometimes we talk about opera, too."

She stared. I don't think she bought it.

A minute later, we crossed another street, hustling to make it across while the sign still flashed WALK.

"My turn," Allison said once we were on the next sidewalk.

"Turn for what?" I said, putting the bag of M&M's back into my pocket.

"My turn for personal questions."

"Um, I think my chauffeur is gonna be here in a minute," I said, pretending to look around for a stretch limousine.

"I'll go easy," she said. "What's your favorite color?"

"Purple."

"Your favorite food?"

"Grapes and pizza," I said. "But not at the same time. I mean, like, I don't put grapes on my pizza."

"Got it. Your favorite musician?"

A chance to be classy again.

"Mozart."

"Really?"

"Beethoven?"

"Uh-huh," she said, not believing me.

"Picasso?"

"You mean Picasso the painter?" she said.

"Yeah, well . . . He played rock guitar, too," I offered.

"Why's your sister hate you?"

"I dunno."

"Oh, come on, you gotta know."

"Really, I don't know." I paused. "Well . . ."

"Well what?" she asked. We made a left and started walking up a street with a lot of big, tall trees.

"Well, I guess she kind of blames me."

"Blames you?" she asked. "For what?"

"For being in seventh grade."

"Huh? How's that your fault?"

"It's not," I said. "But still, she blames me."

I hopped over a puddle made by someone's broken lawn sprinkler. Allison just walked around it.

"I don't understand." She stopped. "This is my

house right here." The house with the broken lawn sprinkler was her neighbor's.

Allison's house looked like most of the other houses in the neighborhood. Nothing too fancy, but not so bad, either. The door was brown and the trim over the front windows was light yellow. A new paint job on the front steps wouldn't have hurt.

"Go ahead," she said. "I'm listening."

I thought she might go inside or something, but nope, she didn't budge. She stood right there waiting to hear my story.

"See, my birthday is in January," I began. "And her birthday is in December, so really, we are less than a year apart. And Hill's smart, one of those good-in-school types, so my parents put us in first grade at the same time, kinda like twins who go to school in the same grade, even though we're not twins."

"Uh-huh . . ."

"So we've been in the same grade our whole lives," I continued. "First, second, third, and so on. All the way up to this year. And for the most part, we always got along."

"Why not this year?"

"Because my sister had a diving accident."

"Like scuba diving?"

"Exactly," I said. "My dad won a raffle at work

and scored a free week at some hotel in the Bahamas, so we all went two summers ago for a vacation and learned how to scuba dive. My sister and I were partnered up."

"The buddy system," Allison said.

"Yeah. You scuba dive?" I asked.

"No, but my dad's taken me snorkeling before. Same principle. Go on."

"So, like, we're down in the water diving and next thing you know my sister gets a piece of seaweed slightly wrapped around her foot—like not even that much at all—and she freaked out. Like, all she had to do was unwrap one little twist, but she panicked and rushed up to the surface too fast, giving her this thing called the bends. You know what the bends are?"

"Nuh-uh."

"It's when too much oxygen goes to your brain because you surfaced too fast. Or maybe it's too much nitrogen, I dunno. Either way, it's like this serious brain thing that can happen from coming up too quick from under the water when you're diving."

"And this happened to your sister?"

"Yeah. So the next year she ended up missing so much time away from class in oxygen tanks and stuff like that trying to get her brain right, they just decided to have her take the entire school year off to recover, get healthy and do seventh grade this year 'cause that's kind of her real age group anyway."

"Is she okay now?" Allison asked.

"Yeah," I said. "We're lucky, she's fine. But she's really mad because . . ."

"Because all her friends are in eighth grade," Allison said.

"Yep. And they're going to the Big Dance, and they're eating during a different lunch period, and blah, blah, blah," I said. "She hates being in seventh grade and blames me for all of it. I just don't get it."

"You don't get it?" Allison asked.

"No, I don't get it."

"Jeez." Allison shook her head. "Boys are so dumb."

"Why am I so dumb?" I asked. But I gotta admit, I said it kinda dumbly.

"You really don't know?"

"Nope, I really don't know."

"Let me ask you," she said. "Where were you when the seaweed got all tangled up around her foot?"

"It wasn't all tangled up," I said. "Don't exaggerate. It was slightly wrapped."

"Answer the question. Where were you?"

"Looking for a clown fish," I said softly.

"Looking for a clown fish?" she repeated.

And don't think I couldn't tell there was a ton of sarcasm in her voice, either.

"Um, hello? You were supposed to be her buddy," Allison said. "You were supposed to be there for her, Bobby."

I guess I'd never really thought of it that way.

"Like I said, boys are so dumb."

She headed for the house.

"Um," I called out from the sidewalk.

"Yes?" she answered in a snippy tone.

"Does my dumbness mean I can't walk you home again tomorrow?" I asked. "I'll bring M&M's."

Allison closed the door without answering. I stood all alone on the sidewalk not knowing what to do.

"Well, does it?" I called out.

No response.

Sheesh, women.

16

When I walked into my house later that afternoon, my sister was sitting at the table wearing a gray hoodie sweatshirt and doing her homework. She looked up when I entered but didn't say hi.

I was dirt to her. Lower than dirt. I was pond scum, the green, slippery kind.

I turned to close the front door behind me but suddenly felt someone pushing it open from the other side.

"Man, we gotta score chicks for the Big Dance," Finkelstein said as he barged in. "By the way, how's your eye?"

"Shut up, Finkelstein," I said. "And hey, why don't you just come right on in?"

"Don't mind if I do. *He-hurrggh, he-hurrggh.*"

Finkelstein leaned his neck out, clearly looking for something. He and my sister made eye contact.

"You couldn't score a chick if one fell out of a truck and hit you on the head," Hill said with a bite.

"Hey, Hill, I hear they invented a new bra for girls with your figure," Finkelstein answered. "It's called the Ironing Board."

"Nice braces, Alfred," Hill replied. "Or did you swallow a pile of bicycle spokes?"

"Toothpick!"

"Chain-link-fence face!"

"Chalkboard chest!"

"Magnet mouth!"

"Will you two shut up!!" I said. "Holy cow, what is it with you two?"

They glared at each other.

"Jeez," I added, and headed upstairs. Finkelstein, of course, followed right behind me.

But not without tossing another dart at Hill.

"Skeleton girl."

"Wire lips."

"Shut up!" I said. "Give it a rest already."

In my room, I discovered Gramps sitting at my computer.

"Ya know, you kids today have it easy," Gramps said. "Back when I was a youngster, if I wanted to see breasts, the best we had was *National Geographic* magazine."

"Are you looking at naked old ladies?" I asked.

"Ever seen this website, Bobby?" he said. "It's

called GargantuanGrandmothers.org. Heck, I ain't never seen gazumbas like these."

"Where?" said Finkelstein, pushing through. "I wanna see."

Finkelstein froze in his tracks.

"Oh my God," Finkelstein shrieked in horror. "Her boobs are wrinkled."

"Lust-worthy, huh?" Gramps said with his yellow-toothed smile.

Finkelstein looked at the screen, practically hypnotized.

"They look like half-inflated beach balls."

"Makes ya feel all electric on the inside, doesn't it?" Gramps said.

Finkelstein turned away, a look of nausea on his face. "I think I'm damaged."

I reached for the computer to turn it off. "My mom checks my site history on this thing, ya know."

"Stop, I'm lookin' at nakedness," Gramps said, pushing my hand away. "Hey, check out this one." He clicked to another webpage. "She's got cantaloupes the size of beanbag chairs."

I grabbed the mouse and closed the browser. Off!

"I thought Gram was coming back today and you were going home," I said.

"She decided to stay a few more days."

Great, I thought. I stared at Gramps for a moment. His hair was uncombed and he was wearing the same pair of blue pajama pants as he did practically every day. Except with underwear. I knew because I could see his tighty-whities popping up from underneath his drooping waistband.

What a mess.

"Hey, Gramps," Finkelstein said, taking a seat on my bed. "How do you score chicks?"

"Don't talk to him, Finkelstein," I said.

"Why not?" Finkelstein said. "I wanna learn from the master."

"Make 'em jealous," Gramps answered. "Ya gotta make 'em jealous."

"And Gramps," I said. "Please don't talk to Finkelstein, either. The two of you should not be communicating with each other. Only bad things will come from it."

"Ah, jealous," Finkelstein said as if a lightbulb of great understanding had just gone off in his head. "You gotta make 'em jealous."

"Exactly," Gramps said. "Girls always want what they cannot have. Make 'em jealous and you'll have hot little tamales lined up by the truckload." Gramps stood up. "Now if you'll excuse me, I gotta go drop the kids off at the pool."

"Drop the kids off at the pool?" Finkelstein asked.

"You know, take a dump," Gramps explained.

"Do I really need to hear this?" I interjected.

"Oh, drop the kids off at the pool," Finkelstein said. "I get it, the toilet. *He-hurrggh, he-hurrggh*."

"You wanna know my three rules for dropping off the kids at the pool, young fella?"

"No, Gramps," I said. "We don't."

"I do," Finkelstein said. I swear those two must have been related in a past life or something.

"First rule for dropping the kids off at the pool," said Gramps.

"He means for taking a poop-ola," Finkelstein said to me as if I was the one who needed it fully explained.

"Shut up, Finkelstein," I said. "And get your feet off my bed."

Finkelstein swung around, rolled onto his stomach and bent his knees so that his legs were shaped like an L.

"Rule number one: No splashing," Gramps said. Finkelstein, his hands under his chin, stared up at my grandfather like it was Storytime Theater.

"Rule number two: No running."

"He-hurggh, he-hurrgh," Finkelstein said to me. "He means diarrhea."

"Finkelstein, I'm gonna break your femur bones," I told him.

"Rule number three," Gramps continued. "Always make sure you bring a towel."

"A towel?" Finkelstein asked. "Oh, you mean toilet paper."

"That's right, youngster," Gramps said, raising his arms so that I got a full shot of the pit stains on his old white T-shirt. "I once copped a squat in the woods and ended up wiping my butt with poison oak. And lemme tell ya, my cornhole itched for a week."

"Can you leave?" I said. "Can both of you just please leave?"

"You don't have to ask me twice," Gramps said. "I think Mr. Turtle is starting to poke his head out of its shell anyway." Gramps reached around and grabbed his rear end like a four-year-old that needed to go potty.

"You too," I said to Finkelstein, grabbing him by the arm. "Leave."

"I like your gramps."

"You're a moron," I said, pulling him toward the door.

"He-hurrggh, he-hurrggh," he laughed. "Wait! I gotta say good-bye to your sister."

Finkelstein pulled away from my grip and headed downstairs. I followed him thinking about that new trail mix my mom had just started buying, the kind with cranberries in it.

"See ya soon, pipe cleaner," Finkelstein said to Hill.

"Try not to eat any more idiot cookies, aluminum breath," she answered. "Oh wait, you already finished the whole box."

"Did not," he said.

"Did too," she replied.

"Did not."

"Did too."

"Did not!"

"Will you two shut up!" I yelled. *Jeez, what is it with them?* I thought. *I mean, what are they, in love or something?*

I stopped.

Oh my goodness.

A moment later, I grabbed the trail mix with the cranberries in it and raced back to my room. I had an idea.

17

The next Monday after dinner, my dad watched the ball game on TV, sitting in his favorite maroon-colored chair with his pants unbuttoned.

"Dad, may I please have eighty dollars?"

"You have a better chance of pulling a violin out of your butt," he answered. "Move, I can't see the game."

Of course a normal kid with a normal parent would just explain to their father why they needed the money. But there's nothing normal about my dad. I knew I had to speak his language.

"Dad, let me rephrase the question for you," I said. "You can either give me eighty dollars, or you can listen to me tell Mom that you look through the binoculars into Mrs. Holston's window every Wednesday night when she's getting dressed for her ballroom dancing class."

My dad almost choked on his beer.

"You wouldn't."

"I would."

"You wouldn't."

"Dad, you can either give me the eighty dollars, or you can talk to Mom about Mrs. Holston's Wednesday night nude-o-rama," I said. "Now what's it gonna be? Make your play."

I stared.

He stared back.

Sure, I was nervous. I'd never really confronted my father like this before. But I needed the money to pull off my idea and I had nowhere else to turn.

He glared, clearly unhappy with the negotiations.

"Are twenties okay?" he finally said, reaching for his wallet.

"Twenties will be fine," I answered.

I think, somewhere deep inside, as he passed me the money, he was actually proud of me. A regular chip off the old block.

"Good decision, Dad. I mean, what would the neighbors think?"

I put the cash in my pocket and went upstairs to work out the rest of my plan. After all, if I could make things better with Hill, that would show Allison I could be a buddy. And if I could show her I could be a buddy, maybe that would also show her I could be—*dare I say it?*—a boyfriend.

Yep, the big enchilada! I was swinging for the fences.

By Tuesday, the Secret Someone invites were flying everywhere.

Samantha Scofield got one. Fat neck Jack Tong got one. Even jerk face Nathan Ox got one.

How Nathan Ox got one, I have no idea. Sure, they say love is blind. But is it deaf, mute and stupid, too?

Nathan didn't even try to pound me in the gonads when he saw me. Instead, he held up his red envelope for all the world to see.

"Big Dance, bay-bee," he said. "The big man is going to the Big Dance!"

Whatever, I thought. I headed off to face down Sheriff Mustache. He was alone at his desk grading papers.

"I'd like to buy four tickets to the Big Dance, please," I said, holding out the money.

He looked up. "You can only buy two."

Why did they have to put him in charge of the tick-ets? I thought.

"But I have money for four," I said, showing him four twenty-dollar bills.

He reached down and grabbed a large, green envelope that contained all the Big Dance tickets.

"Two is the limit."

"But . . ."

"No buts," Sheriff Mustache said, cutting me off. "Mrs. Mank made the rule because two years ago they ran out of tickets and not all the kids could go." He set down his pencil and opened the green envelope. "You want 'em or not?"

"But . . ."

"I said no buts," he told me.

Hmm, what to do? I needed four.

"Look, Bobby, chaperoning the dance is one thing, but being in charge of this stuff is already taking up way too much of my time, so you have about three seconds to make a decision."

"Okay, I'll take two," I said, passing him forty dollars.

"Who are they for?" he then asked, preparing to write something down on a ledger.

"What?" I answered nervously.

"Who are they for?" he asked again.

"Um . . ."

"Anyone I know?" He grew more intimidating by the second. "Anyone I care about?" Sheriff Mustache then rose from his desk, towering over me. He was a guy who had a teacherly look about him, a boring tie with a boring long-sleeve shirt, but he was not an out-of-shape man at all. In fact, Sheriff Mustache looked strong and athletic, like maybe he played sports or something.

Clearly, he could kick my butt.

"Perhaps you're planning to take someone that might make me want to go load bullets into my shotgun?" he commented.

"Y-y-you have a shotgun?"

"All math teachers have shotguns, Bobby. Think about that the next time you don't do homework."

"Can I just have two tickets, please?" I said with a gulp.

He slowly passed me two tickets and two red envelopes. I put everything in my backpack. Sheriff Mustache smiled at me as I hustled out of the room, but I don't know if he was smiling at me because he was just kidding around or if he was smiling at me because he was thinking about how to turn me into meat sauce for his chili.

An hour later I got a boner in science. An hour after that I got a boner in English. An hour after that I got a boner in social studies, but since we were studying different flags from around the world, having a flagpole in my pants didn't really feel so out of place.

No more boners in math, though. Go figure. Not

that I had a clue how to deal with any of them, of course. Perhaps there was an anti-erection ointment of some sort they sold at drugstores, a NO-BONE cream or something?

After school that day, I headed off to Dr. Cox. I walked into her office and set my stuff down on the brown table.

"So," she asked once I was seated, "have you had any erections in school lately?"

"Nope," I told her. "Not a one."

She lowered her thin eyeglasses and looked over the rims of them at me.

"Really?" she said.

"Really," I confirmed.

Clearly, she and I were making lots of progress.

18

After therapy I went home. Hill was floating on cloud nine.

"What's with you?" I said in a snippy tone.

"Oh, nothing." Then she accidentally on purpose pushed a red envelope into the center of the table. I could tell she was dying to tell me, wanting to really rub it in.

I played along. "What's that?" I said with a pretend edge in my voice. There was a bowl of green grapes on the table. I grabbed a few.

She twirled her hair. "Oh, nothing really. Just a Secret Someone invite for me to go to the Big Dance."

"Who's it from?" I asked, lifting it up. But she snatched it away from me, too precious for dirt like me to even touch.

"I don't know," she said. "It's secret."

I hadn't seen Hill this happy since, well, since before the diving accident.

"You can't go to the Big Dance," I said. "You're only in seventh grade."

"For your information," she snapped back, "I can too go to the Big Dance. Only eighth graders can buy tickets, but if an eighth grader invites a seventh grader, they're allowed to go, so there."

Of course, I knew that. I just wanted to throw her off the scent so she wouldn't figure out it was me who bought her the ticket. Because if she did find out, she'd hate me even more than she already did for showing her pity.

"Who sent it to you?" I asked, popping a grape in my mouth. I like red grapes better than green ones. And I've told my mom that about a thousand times, too. She never listens, though.

"I told you, it's a Secret Someone," Hill repeated, as if I were a total idiot. "That means the person won't come forward to reveal themselves until we're at the dance. Don't you know anything? Jeez."

Ticket in hand, she marched off.

Perfect, I thought.

That Thursday, I made sure Mr. Moron got his Secret Someone ticket, too. I wanted to make sure that each of them got their tickets on different days in order to

144

avoid any kind of weird coincidence from spoiling my plan.

"Well, looky here at what this sexy-wexy hunk of manhood got stuck in his locker."

"What are you talkin' about, Finkelstein?" I said like I had no clue.

"Well, it seems some lil' piece of butternut squash finds the sugar in my teapot a bit too tasty not to sip," he said.

"English, Finkelstein," I said. "Speak English."

"Secret Someone invite." He held up a red envelope. "Score!"

"You got a Secret Someone invite?" I said. "I thought you were against Secret Someone invites."

"I am against *me* giving out a Secret Someone invite," he said, putting extra emphasis on the word *me*. "But if a dainty little sheep finds the corn kernels in my bucket too delicious not to tickle, who am I to stand in the way of Mother Nature's law of attraction?"

"Did you fall and hit your head?"

"Aw, don't feel bad, Bobby," Finkelstein said, throwing his arm around my shoulders. "You might still land a nugget for the Big Dance. I mean, not everyone can be a piece of irresistible cheese on the mousetrap of life, if you know what I mean."

"I don't, Finkelstein." I tossed his arm off of me. "I really don't know what you mean." I think my plan to hook up Finkelstein and my sister was working too well. They were both experiencing delusions of grandeur.

"Gotta go, bro," Finkelstein said. "Seeing the orthodontist for tomorrow's big festivities. He's cooking up something special for me."

"What color?" I asked.

"Can't tell ya. It's a surprise," he said. "But I'll give you a hint."

"Forget it," I said. "I don't want a hint. I don't even know why I asked."

"I'll give you a hint," he said.

"I don't want a hint."

"Okay, you talked me into it. Neon!" he said. "Neon with dots and stripes."

"Neon?"

"Uh-huh." He smiled proudly.

"With dots and stripes?" I said. "Finkelstein, why would anybody intentionally put dots and stripes on their teeth?"

"For *sexxxxiness,*" he said. *"Rrrrrrrrrr!"*

Finkelstein then licked his finger and wiped the spit across his eyebrow. I swear that kid was ready for the loony bin.

"Finkelstein, I never thought I'd say this," I told

him, "but considering the circumstances, I think sunrise and carrots is a better option."

"I'm pulling out all the stops, Bobby," he replied. "Tomorrow night for the Big Dance, I am going pedal to the metal." Finkelstein grinned and cruised off.

"Well, make sure you have your head checked, too!" I yelled after him. "A functioning brain might be of some assistance in your future!"

A moment later, however, I forgot all about him, because heading toward me was the best sight a guy like me could ever hope to see.

Allison Summers. Her hair was tied back in a green headband that matched her green T-shirt, which, of course, brought out her green eyes.

"Hi-hi," she said, her face beaming like sunshine.

"Hi-hi." I must have saved a blind, three-legged puppy from a getting hit by a truck in a past life or something. I mean, what explanation other than great karma could there be for me being so ridiculously lucky to have a girl like this in my life?

"You, um, walking home?" I asked.

"Yeah," she replied. "You?"

"Not sure," I answered. "I mean, they want me to join the after-school nuclear physics team."

"The after-school nuclear physics team?"

"Yeah," I told her. "But with my jujitsu class and

the cake-decorating course I already signed up for, well . . . sometimes it can be a bit much."

"You decorate cakes, too?" she said with a grin.

"Not weddings," I answered. "Just birthdays, graduations and anniversaries. Weddings don't present enough of a challenge."

"Oh. I see."

"But now that I think about it," I told her, "walking you home is probably best for my bionic foot anyway."

"You have a bionic foot?"

"Not one hundred percent," I answered. "My toes are real."

She laughed. How awesome was it that Dr. Cox had some sort of personal emergency that had forced her to cancel our regular Thursday after-school session? Talk about an awesome break.

Allison tore open a bag of peanut M&M's as we walked along.

"Oh, you came prepared, I see."

She popped a blue M&M into her mouth.

"For me, maybe, not for you," she teased, not offering me any. A moment later she smiled, then poured a few peanut M&M's into my hand.

"You got our tickets to the Big Dance, right?"

"Of course," I answered. "Of course."

Okay, so technically I still didn't have *our* tickets. But I did have the money for the tickets and that was the biggest part of getting tickets anyway, right? All I really needed to do was figure out how to get her father, Sheriff "You Can Only Buy Two Tickets" Mustache, to sell 'em to me.

Right then it hit me. I could get another kid who wasn't going to the dance to buy the tickets for me. But who?

Stephanie Teemer. Of course!

I mean, her parents were so religious they didn't believe eighth graders should be going to dances anyway, so I knew Stephanie wouldn't be able to attend. Plus, we'd done good business with each other before. I felt pretty confident that eighteen boxes of Mentos and a wheelbarrow full of Jawbreakers would do the trick.

Besides, when I peeked at Sheriff Mustache's green envelope the other day, it looked as if there were still about twenty thousand tickets left. I betcha he was just making up that stuff about Mrs. Mank's two-ticket rule just because he didn't like me.

Good idea, Bobby. I decided to hit up Stephanie on the school's e-chat system as soon as I got home.

Things were working out great!

The only thing I wasn't too sure about right then

was whether or not to tell Allison about my great plan to set my sister up with a way to go to the Big Dance and party with all her friends.

After all, I didn't want Allison to think that I was just being nice to my sister simply so that I could score points with her. But on the other hand, I was definitely hoping that by being nice to my sister I was gonna score points with her.

Hmm, what to do? Should I come right out and tell her, or should I hang back and wait for the exact right moment to appear?

I decided to wait.

My plan was a good one. Allison would go to the Big Dance, Hill would go to the Big Dance, and Finkelstein would go to the Big Dance, and by the time it was over I'd have fixed my relationship with my sister, found someone else to occupy Finkelstein's time, and landed my first real girlfriend.

Nice. The universe was humming along.

I looked around for a kitten to assist or maybe a toothless squirrel that needed some help opening a nut in order to keep my good karma going, but didn't see any opportunities. Oh, well, if any animals needed my assistance, I could give them my phone number or something.

Along the way to her house, Allison and I talked

about school stuff. We chatted about teachers with bad breath, dumb lunch-line rules, and how cool the school librarian, Mrs. Meredith, was. Mrs. M, as all the kids called her, was always trying to bring interesting stuff into our school. A few months ago she even did a special program on banned books, explaining how censorship was a bunch of baloney.

"I mean, isn't the point of education to get kids like us to think about these things for ourselves?" Allison asked, getting all serious about the banned books issue. "Really, it's not like we're not going to grow up one day. Admit it, Mrs. M rocks."

"I like how last month she told us about how doctors are using video games to warm up for surgery," I said. "I went right home and told my mom that I needed to spend more hours playing Die Death Die so I could get into medical school."

"Did she buy it?"

"She made me water the plants."

Allison laughed. Before I knew it we had polished off two bags of M&M's—I had brought one, too—and arrived at her door.

"Wanna come in?" she asked.

I paused. There was a silver car in the driveway. That could only mean one thing: Sheriff Mustache.

"You mean, like, into your house?" I asked.

"Um, yeah," she replied. "You have been in a person's house before, haven't you?"

"Well, um . . ." I glanced a second time at the car in the driveway, not sure of how to say what I was thinking.

"Oh, my dad?" she said, also looking at the silver vehicle. She checked her watch. "It's his daily jog time. Does it religiously. He's not home now."

"He's not?" I said. "And still I can . . . I can still come in?"

"Of course," she answered. "My dad trusts me."

"Wow," I said. "I wonder what that feels like."

She reached for her key.

"Trust is everything, Bobby. If I don't trust someone, I don't deal with them. It's one of my rules."

"You have rules?" I asked.

"I have rules," she answered, putting her key in the lock.

"What kind of rules?"

"Like, be a giver," she said.

"Be a giver?" I said, not quite understanding. I mean, I had rules, too. I guess. Like never eating yellow snow and making sure to wipe my butt after going number two, but for some reason I didn't think these were the same kind of rules she was talking about.

"Yep, be a giver," she repeated. "Give to people who need your help. That's how my mom passed away. She was flying to Ecuador to do some aid work for a group called Doctors Without Borders and there was a plane crash."

"A plane crash?" I said.

"Yeah," Allison said, opening the door. "Going to therapy really helped me work some of the issues out."

"You mean you used to see a shrink?" I asked.

"Still do," she said. "I mean, whenever I feel I want to talk. My therapist helped me to understand some stuff. About myself, about my mom. I mean, like, she died giving. I used to be really angry about that, but then realized that giving to others was important to her. I guess that's why being a giver is also important to me."

Oh my goodness, I thought. *Wait till she finds out about me hooking up my sister with a date for the dance. I am SO in, bay-beeeee!*

Right then I decided to tell her everything.

"You know, I—"

"But the other thing I learned about my mom by talking to my therapist was," she continued, "that you should really only do good deeds for the sake of the deed itself, not for the credit. I don't like it when people do things just to get the credit for them. That's kinda wrong."

Gulp.

"Sorry, didn't mean to interrupt. Were you gonna say something?"

"Me, um . . . no. I mean, yes. I mean . . . nice door."

She turned her head sideways. "Nice door?"

"You have a nice front door," I said, standing in the archway. "It's very . . . door-y."

"Door-y?"

"Yeah, door-y," I said. "You know how some doors aren't really that door-y? Well, yours is."

"Uh, yeah, right," she said. "So, are you comin' inside or what?"

"Inside? Does that, um, mean you trust me?" I said with a smile.

"No," she answered. "It means I trust me."

She grinned and I followed her in.

Allison's house was nice. At least the living room was. There was a tan couch with a leather reclining chair and a fireplace in the front room. A small pile of wood was neatly stacked next to the fireplace, but since the weather had been pretty warm the past few weeks, I doubted they had used it in a while.

Allison dropped her backpack by a briefcase that was already sitting on the coffee table.

"You want something to drink? There's apple juice."

"No, thanks," I said. "I'm fine."

"Well, if you change your mind, the kitchen is in there. Help yourself. I'm gonna change real quick," she said. "Wait here," she added as she headed for the stairs. "I mean, my dad trusts me, but he doesn't trust me that much."

"Gotcha," I said.

I sat on the couch and waited.

Looking around the living room, I saw all the regular stuff you usually see in living rooms. Family pictures, a couple of candles, a set of coasters, the green envelope with the Big Dance tickets on the coffee table, the remote control for the TV, a—

The green envelope with the Big Dance tickets?

Hmm. I looked around. I was the only one in the room.

Maybe I didn't need Stephanie Teemer? I mean what if I took two tickets, put the money for them in the envelope and *poof,* problem solved.

Wow, when it came to solving predicaments, the universe sure worked fast for me. For sure I was going to aid an ailing giraffe or mend the paw of a limping coyote or something when I got home tonight. The universe was just being way too good to me.

I listened for signs of someone coming. Coast was clear. Quick like a cat, I opened the green envelope and sure enough, there were about seventy or eighty Big Dance tickets inside, as well as a thick wad of cash.

Sheriff Mustache would never know.

I swapped two dance tickets for two twenty-dollar bills. Carefully, I mixed the twenties into the wad of cash that was already there and wrapped it all together.

There must have been hundreds of dollars in my hand. Maybe even a thousand? I'd never held so much money in all my life.

But I would never steal it. I wasn't even tempted. That just wasn't the type of person I was.

I carefully put the green envelope back just the way I'd found it and tucked the two tickets into my pocket.

There, I thought. *Like a ninja warrior at midnight.*

There was still no sign of Allison. Why did girls always take so long to get changed? Me, I could be in and out of an outfit in less than eighteen seconds . . .

and that's with having my shoes tied. But girls, with them two minutes always meant a hundred hours.

What was she doing, knitting herself a new sweatshirt?

I decided to go for the apple juice. I mean, I wasn't really all that thirsty, but at least it would give me something to do. Better than staring at a fireplace without a fire.

I went to the kitchen and opened the fridge.

Vegetables. Whole grain bread. Apple juice. I took out the container. It was one of those super-big jugs, the kind that you can only buy at warehouse stores. I needed two hands just to lift the darn thing, it was so heavy. Jeez, how many gallons of apple juice did two people need?

I unscrewed the top and then opened the kitchen cabinet, searching for a glass.

Plates. Wrong cabinet.

Bowls. Wrong cabinet.

Ah, glasses. I grabbed one. They felt like the expensive kind. I reached up to close the cabinet and then, suddenly, heard a voice.

"Sweetie, I'm home."

Oh no, Sheriff Mustache! What was he doing here? And what was I doing in his kitchen?

Quick, back to the living room, I thought.

That's when it all fell apart.

When I turned to dash back to the couch, I—*oh crap!!*—knocked over the glass.

Everything from that point on happened so quickly, even though I saw it all go down in slow motion.

I knocked over the glass.

I reached for the glass.

I didn't get to the glass in time.

The glass fell to the ground, nothing I could do.

CRASH!! Broken glass everywhere.

But worse, while trying to catch the falling glass, my elbow knocked over the giant container of apple juice.

SPLASH!! A spill. The entire thirty-gallon bottle.

All over the floor. All over the counter. It even splashed up inside the open refrigerator door.

A total catastrophe.

At the sound of all the noise Sheriff Mustache rushed into the kitchen.

"Sweetie, are you okay?"

He froze when he saw me.

"Um, hi, Mr. Summers."

Sheriff Mustache slowly checked out the mess. He was wearing running clothes and sneakers, his muscular shoulders wet with sweat. The black hair of his chest popped over the low collar of his damp Reebok tank top.

"Did you, um, have a nice jog, sir?" I asked.

He squinted.

Juice dripped from the counter to the floor. Pieces of broken glass lay everywhere. Allison was nowhere in sight.

We both looked down at the same time to see a puddle turn into a stream. Suddenly, a river of apple juice began to flow beneath his refrigerator, to that place that no one can ever get to.

Gulp!

"You know, that was a really good math class today." I made my voice cheery. "A very solid lesson plan. I mean, who knew fractions could be so interesting."

Sheriff Mustache growled, part man, part werewolf.

19

The next day at school, the entire eighth grade buzzed about the Big Dance. It was all anyone could think about.

Me included.

Sure, it'd be held in the school gym, but who cared. The dance—not the location of the dance—was what mattered. Chips, pretzels, soda pop, some tables, chairs and a coupla streamers in our school colors to decorate the place were all we needed. The rest, Mother Nature would take care of that.

I just hoped Mother Nature wouldn't take care of sending me a terribly timed, out-of-the-blue bone-a-rooskie, too. I shook my head, banished the thought from my brain and searched the halls for Allison before class started, just wanting to say hi-hi. But I couldn't find her.

After first period, no sight.

After second period, no sight.

During Nutrition Break, I raced to the center of the main hall and waited. I was sure she'd cross through on her way to science class.

"Wanna hear my most brilliant poem yet?"

"No," I said, trying to peek over the heads of all the students passing through the halls.

"It's called 'Boogers, Belly Button Lint and Toe Fungus.'"

"You're disgusting, Finkelstein."

"Oh, how wrong you are, my friend," he answered. "When the sugar bear hears me whisper my words of romance tonight, she's gonna melt like cheddar cheese on a buffalo burger."

"You think a poem about toe fungus is gonna impress a girl?" I asked.

"Three words, Bobby," said Finkelstein. "I'll be tasting taste buds."

"That's five, you moron."

"He-hurrrgh, he-hurrggh, I know."

Lots of kids cruising past to the left and right but still, there was no sight of Allison. "You really are a mental case, you know that, Finkelstein?"

"You do yours yet?"

"My what? My poem? Nah, been busy."

"You better get on it, Bobby. It's due soon."

"Yeah, yeah," I said, straining my neck to make sure I checked every kid in the crowd. Just then, I spied her. "Hey, Allison, wait."

She cruised past at full speed without bothering to acknowledge me, even though I was sure she'd heard me.

"Like, what's up with that?" I said.

"Aw," said Finkelstein. "The little sesame seedsicle will come around, Bobby. The jealous ones always do."

"Seedsicle?" I said. A few girls passed between me and Finkelstein talking about, what else, the Big Dance.

"Yeah, seedsicle," he answered once the girls had walked through. "It's a good word. Scores high in Yahtzee."

"You mean Scrabble."

"Same thing," he said.

"Finkelstein, you're a moron." I gazed down the hall wondering if Allison was going to turn around or not.

"Well, if I am such a moron, how come my plan is working to perfection?" he asked.

"What plan?" I said. "What are you talking about, Finkelstein?"

"My plan to get my best friend his little sesame

seedsicle," he answered. "I mean, why do you think Allison is pretending to be mad at you?"

"I don't think she's pretending." Allison had vanished into a sea of kids. "In fact, I'm thinkin' she might have found out about something I did."

"She didn't find out about nothin'," Finkelstein said confidently. "Trust me, she's pretending. And you know why?"

"I don't know why."

"Do you want to know why?"

"Please, tell me why."

"Why should I tell you why . . . said Mr. Fly as he said bye-bye to the guy with the eye that looked like a pie?" Finkelstein answered. "Ow! Stop, Bobby, let go."

"Talk, Finkelstein," I ordered. "Now!"

"She's mad because I told the lil' cucumber sandwich you were going to the dance with Jenny McNeil tonight."

"You told her what?" I said, letting Finkelstein go.

"It's like Gramps said," he told me. "Ya gotta make 'em jealous. They all want what they cannot have, and I knew how much you wanted to go with her, so I did you a favor."

"A favor?" I said, trying to think this through. "When did you tell her this?"

"Today," he answered. "Right before first period."

No wonder she'd been avoiding me all morning. I raced off to go catch up with Allison before she went into her science class. I caught sight of the red sweater only after weaving in and out of a few zillion people.

But just then someone grabbed me from behind.

"We missed our appointment yesterday."

Oh no, I thought.

"Look," I said, turning around. "I don't have time to talk right now. See, I have to—"

"Your time is my time, Bobby," replied Dr. Cox. "And I need to have a session."

"*You* need to have a session?"

"I mean I need you to have a rescheduled session," she said, rephrasing her words. "You know, because I had to cancel."

"When? Now?"

"Yes," she answered, adjusting her thin eyeglass frames. "Right now."

"But . . ." Allison's red sweater faded further into the distance. "I can't," I said. "I . . . um . . . I have class in, like, three minutes."

I made a move to dash off, but she grabbed my arm.

"I'll write you a pass."

"But—"

"Look, Bobby," she began. Dr. Cox looked flustered and kinda weirded out. Her neck was covered today by a white turtleneck sweater, but it was sleeveless and I could still see every vein in her pencil-thin arms. "I've had a really hard day and I don't want to do anything rash, but if you do not come with me right now to do as you are obligated, I'll have no choice but to consider you in violation of your probationary agreement and make the recommendation to have you expelled from this school."

"Expelled?" I said, shocked by the words.

She nodded. "Expelled."

I looked down the hall. The red sweater was gone, having disappeared into a soup of students.

I took a moment to think about it. Dr. Cox was just nutty enough to have me kicked out of school even though I really hadn't done anything to deserve it. And our vice principal certainly wasn't going to take my side of the story over hers.

Maybe my parents would have my back?

Yeah, right. I dropped my head.

"Lead the way."

"Good decision, Bobby," she replied. "Good decision."

A few minutes later, we took our usual seats in her office, me on the couch, her in the upright office chair.

"Look, I'm sorry about back there," she began. "It's just been a tough day, you know?"

I didn't answer.

"I mean, I just don't understand why I always fall for the wrong guy," she continued. "It's like I'm a magnet for losers or something. Really, why do I always choose men who are afraid of commitment?"

What the heck is she talking about?

"Or liars," she continued. "Oh, do I love the liars. I mean, come on, I should have known by the way he always carries that bullhorn around and thinks he's so much more superior than all the students that things weren't going to work out with this one."

Carries his bullhorn? Is she talking about Mr. Hildge?

"Oh yeah, always the losers for me," she complained. "Always the losers."

Dr. Cox gazed off in the distance with a faraway look in her eyes. A moment later, she took off her eyeglasses and began to rub her temples.

"You know, I think it goes back to my own feelings of inadequacy surrounding my father." She stood up and walked over to me.

"Huh?"

"You know, the role of the paternal in the formulation of an adolescent's psyche is one of the most critical components to healthy childhood develop-ment," she said. "It's in all the research. Mind if I sit?"

"'Scuse me?"

She scooched me off the couch. We had traded places—I was now in the chair.

"You know, Bobby, you're the only one who takes me seriously on this campus. Every other kid I see thinks I am a joke."

Dr. Cox reclined.

"Of course my dad wasn't good with intimacy." With her head back, she looked up at the ceiling. "I never remember him hugging me, you know? Like really hugging me."

For the next forty-five minutes Dr. Cox blabbered on about her feelings of insecurity, about how she always just wanted male approval in her life and about a rocking horse that had really traumatized her when she was in middle school. I had no idea what she was talking about.

But the longer she talked, the worse she got.

"And then," she said with tears streaming down her face, "after all that, I still didn't get the yellow doll. Can you believe that? How could they not get me the yellow doll? Didn't they know how much the yellow doll meant to me?"

It took her three full boxes of tissues before she

finally told me I could leave her office. As soon as she wrote me out a hall pass on official school stationery, I was gone.

I caught up with Allison just before the bell to begin fifth period was about to ring.

"Hi-hi," I said.

"What, Bobby?" Allison replied.

No hi-hi, I thought. Oh boy, she was mad.

"What?" she repeated.

"We need to talk," I said.

"No, we don't, Bobby. We don't need to talk at all. Ever."

Allison walked away. Suddenly, I felt a chin rest itself on my shoulder.

"Oh, the tiny little cream cookie is gonna be saying gobble, gobble, gobble in no time at all. Ya got her right where you want her, Bobby boy. Right where you want her."

"Shut up, Finkelstein," I said, pushing him away. I dashed off to catch back up to Allison.

"Allison, wait," I said. "Don't be mad. I'm not going with Jenny to the dance. I swear, I'm going with you."

"No, you're not," she replied.

"But Finkelstein was just making that stuff up so that—"

"That's not why I'm mad, Bobby," she said, spinning around to face me. "I'm mad because you stole the tickets."

"Stole the tickets? I didn't steal the tickets. I—"

"I don't want to hear it, Bobby." She walked off again.

"But Allison," I pleaded, chasing after her. "You don't understand—"

"I don't want to hear it, Bobby. My dad knows it was you."

"But Finkelstein and my sister—"

"Bobby!" Her cheeks were red hot. "Just answer one question: Did you or did you not take two tickets from the green envelope when you were at my house yesterday?"

"You don't understand, I . . ."

"It's a yes or no question, Bobby," she said. "When you were at my house yesterday—I don't even know why I'm asking 'cause all the tickets are numbered and my dad knows who bought which ones anyway, but humor me—did you or did you not go into the green envelope?"

"But I . . ."

"No buts, Bobby. Yes or no?"

"But you see, I . . ."

"Yes or no, Bobby?" She put her hands on her hips. "Did you or did you not go into the green envelope?"

I stood there like a block of wood.

"Yes or no?"

Her eyes were laser beams. There was a long silence.

"Yes," I said softly, lowering my head.

"I thought I could trust you," she replied. The words practically burned a hole through my heart. "Good-bye."

"But—"

"Good-bye!" she repeated. "And don't ever talk to me again."

She stormed off. Finkelstein approached a second later.

"Worked like a charm, right, Bobby boy?" he said with a big, goofy grin. "The lil' coffee cup just needs a few vanilla beans and then—"

"Leave me alone, Finkelstein." I slowly shuffled away.

"Aw, don't be like that, Bobby," Finkelstein said, catching up. "It's all going perfect according to the master plan."

"Shut up, Finkelstein."

"Hey, bro," he said. "You just need some faith that the jelly jam you're planning for the toast parade is—"

"I mean it!" I said. "Shut up! You're an idiot, you know that? A total and complete idiot."

"He-hurrgh, He-hurrgh."

"I'm being serious, Finkelstein." My anger grew. "Look at you. You're a bozo. And you do nothing but annoy the crap out of me," I said. "Really, you do. You're like a genuine loser in life and the truth is, I wish you would just leave me alone."

His shoulders sank and the grin disappeared from his face.

"Stay out of my life, okay? We're not friends. We're not buddies. We're not nothing," I said. "I mean, how in the world can I make this more clear to you?" I leaned in close. "You're a moron. Stay away," I said. "Just stay one hundred percent away!"

The bell rang. Next period for me? Math class, of course.

I left Finkelstein in the middle of the hall. After a deep breath, I opened the door to class and slipped quietly into my assigned seat.

"Take out a pencil," Sheriff Mustache ordered all of his students. "Time for the Friday quiz."

Sheriff Mustache walked up and down the aisles

171

handing each student a test. I looked at Allison. I'm sure she felt my eyes on her, but she didn't turn around. When Sheriff Mustache finally got to me, he put a piece of paper facedown on my desk, but instead of walking on, he stopped.

"You have some nerve, Bobby," he said in a low, deep voice. "You know that? Some incredible nerve."

20

I sat at the kitchen table making train tracks in my mashed potatoes with my fork. I hadn't eaten a thing. Hadn't even sipped my milk.

Behind me, dancing around in the brand-new yellow dress my mother had just bought her, was Hill.

"Can I just say how excited I am to meet my Secret Someone? Like, wow!" She twirled around.

"Yeah," I said. "Bet he's gonna be just gorgeous."

"Shut up, Bobby," Hill snapped. "What do you know?"

"Dots and stripes," I said under my breath.

"What?"

"Nothin'," I said. "Nothin'."

Boy, was she in for a letdown. I pulled an envelope from my backpack.

"Just give this to Allison for me, okay?" I said, holding out the envelope for Hill to take.

"Who's Allison?"

"She's that new math teacher's daughter." I'd heard Jamie Parker tell Bonnie Johnson that Allison's father was making her go to the Big Dance even though she didn't want to. Sheriff Mustache had to be there to chaperone, so Allison was going whether she wanted to or not.

"Just do it, okay?"

She took the envelope and thoughtlessly shoved it into her purse.

"Whatever," she said.

I brought my plate into the kitchen, scraped the uneaten chow into the garbage, then headed for my room. On my way back through the living room, my dad shook his head in a "tsk-tsk" type of way.

"What?" my mom said to him.

"Second-class folks chasing first-class goods," he replied, looking at me. "It'll break your heart every time."

"Excuse me?" Mom was lost.

"Nothing, honey," Dad answered. "Just remembering the reason I married you, dear, that's all."

Dad smiled.

"And why's that?" Mom asked, putting her hands on her hips.

"Because we're right for each other, honey. You and I are right for each other."

Mom grinned and gave him a little peck on the cheek. Dad then winked at me.

What a jerk. My whole stupid life was filled with jerks.

Suddenly, a car horn beeped outside. One of Hill's eighth grade friends, Zoe Elkins, had come to pick her up for the giant event. Hill practically glowed from the idea of getting her old life, and her old friends, back. At least for a night.

"Bye, Mom," Hill shouted as she grabbed her purse. The door slammed. Hill was on her way to the Big Dance.

And I wasn't.

I looked at my dad one more time. He shook his head and gave me an "I told you so" look.

And who doesn't love getting those? I went to my room, shoulders slumped.

When I opened my bedroom door, my grandfather was standing stark naked in front of the window. His wrinkled, flabby butt stared at me.

"What are you doing?" I exclaimed.

"Ventilating," Gramps replied, turning around.

I quickly covered my eyes before I saw his willy. The last thing I needed right then was a full frontal view of my three-hundred-year-old grandfather's over-ripe banana.

"It's good to get some fresh air on your weenie every once in a while," he said to me. "Besides, Mr. Friendly enjoys the great outdoors."

"For goodness' sake, put on some clothes, will ya, Gramps?"

"All right, all right." He reached for his underwear, a pair of tighty-whities that were torn at the waist. When I get to be a crazy old man, I hope someone just shoots me.

"Why do you always have to do this freaky stuff in my room?"

"Well, you're in some mood, huh?" he asked. "This got something to do with that hot little tamale your dad said just dumped you?"

"She wasn't a tamale. She was a person!" I snapped. "A nice person that I really, really liked and now she hates me, okay? Jeez, people aren't food, ya know, Gramps!"

I crossed the room and slammed my window closed. I was sick and tired of my grandfather always being such a . . . I don't know.

Such a putz!

"But how would you know about that anyway?" I continued. "I mean, you're pathetic. To you, people are tamales or tomatoes or whatever other stupid food things you call them. But I cared about Allison and now I blew it. I totally blew it and I lost her."

I threw my curtains closed.

"And that sucks. To me, that really, really sucks!"

I waited for a smart-aleck response. I was sure he'd have some stupid, offensive or insulting thing to say. But instead of responding with a wisecrack, Gramps got quiet, and it was a long moment before he spoke.

"She kicked me out."

"What?" I said. "What are you talking about? Who?"

"Your grandmother," he said, slumping into a chair. "She kicked me out."

When Grandpa Ralph looked up at me, his eyes were bloodshot.

"I'm not here for a few more days, Bobby," Gramps admitted. "I got nowhere to go." He sniffled. "You think you blew it? I'm the one who blew it. I screwed things up with the most important person in my life, the person I just spent the past fifty-four years with."

He ran his fingers through his uncombed hair.

"I guess she finally got sick and tired of me acting like a jackass, flirting with all the young girls, making stupid comments every chance I got, stuff like that," he said. "So she gave me the boot. And can you blame her? Can you really blame her?"

A tear fell from his eye.

"She was my dream girl," he said. "She was the honest-to-goodness best thing that ever happened to me. And I took her for granted. Acted like an idiot. And I lost her. I lost her, Bobby."

He started to cry. Really cry. I stared at him, not knowing what to say.

"You know, you're right, I am pathetic," he said. "I'm nothing but a pathetic, sad old man. A fool."

Gramps sat there weeping in the chair. I'd never seen him like this before. I had never once seen him act like, well . . . like a real person with feelings.

He sniffled some more. As he hunched over, I noticed, for the first time, how much he and my father looked alike.

I mean they really looked alike. The way their eyes were set. The way their foreheads sloped. The size of their noses.

I looked in the mirror and saw how I kind of looked like them, too. People had always said so my whole life. All three of us had the same dimpled chin.

"Get up, Gramps," I said, grabbing him under the arm.

"Why?"

"Because you gotta go get her," I said.

He pulled his arm away. "Forget it, Bobby. She's gone."

"She's not gone, Gramps," I said. "And neither is Allison. Together, we're gonna go win back our girls. Come on, stand up."

"Go without me, Bobby. My chance is gone," Gramps said. "I'm just gonna sit here and blow farts till they throw me in an old persons' home and feed me Jell-O."

"Stop talking like that," I said, trying to lift him up again. "We're going. Now!"

"What the hell has gotten into you?" he asked.

"My father," I said.

Gramps wrinkled his forehead, not understanding.

"I never want to be like him," I answered. "And really, Gramps, neither do you."

He thought about it. Suddenly, I saw a light in his eyes.

"You know what? You're right. Pass me some underwear, Bobby," he ordered as he rose to his feet. "Let's do it!"

"Um, Gramps," I said. "You're already wearing underwear."

"I know." He crossed the room and opened my drawer. "But I like to double up and yours provides good support for Mr. Dongster."

He put a pair of my undies on over the ones he was already wearing.

"You've been wearing my underwear?"

"Not on the outside," Gramps answered. "Usually I wear them on the inside, but I figure we're in a rush, so I'm trying to dress quickly."

Uggh. He readjusted my tighty-whities.

"Best thing about 'em," he said, "is that when I'm done, I just throw 'em right back in the drawer. Cuts down on the laundry for your mother that way."

"Okay," I said. "Freaking out over here."

"So tell me," Gramps said, hoisting up his pants. "What's the plan?"

"Can you drive?" I asked.

"I lost my license seventeen years ago for running a red light."

"They take away your license for running red lights?" I asked.

"They do when you're going a hundred and seventeen miles per hour down the sidewalk," he answered. "I'm not so good in traffic," he confessed.

Hmm. I thought about it for a sec. "But you can drive without killing us, right?"

"You mean, if I had a car, could I drive without killing us? Yeah, I think so," he answered.

Two minutes later Gramps and I were standing in front of my father. "Dad," I said. "We need the car."

"No chance," he answered. "Move. I can't see the TV." Some stupid bowling championship had him riveted. "This guy's only two strikes away from a three hundred."

"A perfect game?" said Mom as she folded a load of towels on the couch. Though she'd been sitting in the room, she hadn't really been paying attention to the TV.

"But Dad . . . ," I said.

"No way, Bobby," he replied. "And don't try to negotiate with me, either. I'm not in the mood."

"Phillip," Gramps said in a firm, fatherly tone. "You can either give me the car keys or you can have your son watch me kick your little ass."

"Gramps, please don't use the A-word," Mom said.

"Eat a lemon, Ilene!" Gramps snapped. "It's crazy the way you two are raisin' these kids. Now gimme the keys, Phillip, before I lay some thunder on ya."

"Calm down, Pop."

Gramps started rolling up his sleeves. "Ya know, it's been a few years since I dropped a man, but I betcha I can still whup your wussy little butt. You always were one of those mousy, whiny twit kids, anyway."

Gramps raised his fists.

"Defend yourself, son."

Grandpa Ralph positioned himself in a boxing stance, his left foot slightly ahead of his right, his shoulders at an angle. To him, this was about winning back the woman he loved and he was going to turn his son's face into pumpkin pie if he dared to stand in the way.

Fear spread across my father's face. Twenty seconds later, Gramps was holding the car keys.

"I hope you have insurance on this vehicle," Gramps said as we left. "Hate to see you sued for giving an unlicensed driver the keys to your ride, Phillip."

Gramps reached into his pocket, popped an orange jelly bean into his mouth and flashed his yellow teeth. Mom looked horrified.

"Ha!" he shouted as he closed the front door behind us. "That'll learn 'em."

We approached our white, four-door Toyota Camry. It wasn't a luxury vehicle by any stretch of the imagination, but my dad kept it clean and crisp.

"Here," Gramps said, suddenly tossing me the keys. "You drive."

"Me?" I said. "I don't know how to drive a car."

"You gotta learn sometime, Bobby," Gramps answered. "I mean, if we're gonna go out, we should go out with a bang, right?"

He flashed another yellow-toothed smile. There was warmth and caring in his eyes.

I looked at the keys.

"Screw it!" I threw open the driver's door, climbed inside and turned over the ignition. The engine roared.

And roared.

And ROARED!

"Um, Bobby, you don't want to keep your foot all the way down on the gas pedal before you even put the car in gear," Gramps suggested.

"Gotcha," I said.

The roaring stopped.

My parents peeked through the front window, nervously looking through the blinds. I put the car in gear and turned to look over my shoulder so I could back out of the driveway.

The car zipped forward and slammed into our garage door.

BAM!

"Oops."

Gramps pointed at the dashboard. "See that little *R*? It stands for reverse. The *D* is for drive."

"Gotcha."

The sound of the car crashing into the garage door was loud enough to frighten Mrs. Holston. She rushed out of her house wearing a red apron and holding a long cooking spoon. Her thoughts were written all over her face.

What in the world is Bobby Connor doing driving an automobile?

Gramps waved.

"Hey there, neighbor. Looking kinda hot! Maybe I'll come over and show you my cooking utensil sometime."

He winked. Mrs. Holston's jaw dropped in shock.

"All right, kid," Gramps said to me. "Let's go."

I looked at the garage door. It was dented badly.

"Oh my goodness," Gramps said in a high-pitched tone. "What will the neighbors think?" He laughed.

As I put the car in reverse and slowly backed out of the driveway, I thought about how I was gonna be grounded till I was thirty-seven years old.

The drive to school and the Big Dance was really slow. And really fast. And really slow . . . and really fast. Sometimes I was doing three miles per hour, sometimes I was doing eighty-seven.

Getting used to the gas pedal took some time. The brakes, however, I got used to right away.

I just slammed on 'em.

Gramps and I were thrown forward and back like rag dolls. If it wasn't for our seat belts, we both woulda been shot through the front windshield twenty times over.

Steering was easy, though. Video games had taught me that. After crossing a few yellow lines, nearly running over an old woman (who clearly had the right-of-way) and hitting eleven orange cones in a construction zone, I felt like I was getting the hang of things. My only real big mistake was turning left down a one-way street, but Gramps wasn't too concerned.

"When you think about it," he said to me as I drove against traffic, "we *are* only going one way."

"Good point," I answered as someone gave me the bird.

We arrived at the Big Dance in one piece. Dad's car did as well. The first bump into the garage door was the only bump.

"Where should I park?" I asked.

"By the fire hydrant," Gramps answered, pointing to my left.

"But Dad might get a ticket," I said.

"If we're lucky," Gramps answered. "Only if we're lucky."

I laughed and pulled into the no-parking zone.

"You did good, Bobby," Gramps said as we walked

up to the front entrance of school. "You practiced the rule of 'no contact' driving. Hard to ask for much more than that your first time out, right?"

"Thanks, Gramps."

He gave me a small pat on the head. It felt nice to be encouraged instead of discouraged for once.

Though my mom had scored me a nice navy-blue suit and dashing yellow tie to wear to the Big Dance, I wasn't wearing it because I really hadn't planned on going till just a few minutes before we left the house. I looked down. Jeans, sneakers and a zip-up sweatshirt. *Great,* I thought. *Prince Charming.* At least Gramps had ditched the blue pajama pants for tan trousers and a long-sleeve beige shirt, though he still hadn't combed his hair in a month.

"So," Gramps said as we headed toward the gymnasium, "what's this little hot tamal . . . I mean, what's your friend Allison look like anyway?"

"She kinda looks like . . ."

Suddenly, a dark shadow appeared in front of us, stopping me dead in my tracks.

"Going somewhere, Bobby?"

I looked up. Sheriff Mustache, dressed in a black suit with a striped red tie.

Gulp.

"Indeed we are," Gramps answered. "We're going in, so move aside, peckerhead."

"Um, Gramps . . ."

"No, Bobby, I got this," Gramps said. "I mean, the last thing I'm going to let happen right now is have some pencilhead school putz stand in our way."

"But Gramps—"

"Bobby, please, let me handle this." Gramps stepped in front of me in a fearless, no-one-is-gonna-mess-with-me-tonight manner. "I can't stand twerps like this anyway," Gramps said to Sheriff Mustache. "Let me guess, you're some kind of power-hungry, scare-all-the-students teacher who gets his silly kicks from bossing around little schoolkids. Am I close, Bobby? Is this guy some sort of campus dictator who spends his entire life trying to make the lives of young people like you miserable because he has a small penis?"

Gramps laughed at the thought of it.

"Hey, pal," Gramps said. "You one of those men with TPS—tiny pecker syndrome?"

"Um, Gramps," I said.

"Yeah, Bobby?"

"That's Allison's father."

He paused.

"Oh." Gramps smiled. "Nice to meet you, sir. Bobby tells me many fine things about your daughter."

Sheriff Mustache's face was so red I thought steam was going to blow out of his ears.

"Jelly bean?" Gramps offered. He reached into his pocket and pulled out a few green, red and yellow candies. "Don't mind the lint, it doesn't digest. You'll poop it right out."

I looked inside the gym and saw Allison walking toward some tables that had been covered with purple plastic tablecloths.

"Allison!" I called out. "Wait!"

She scowled at me, then walked on.

I made a move to go after her, but Sheriff Mustache grabbed me.

"You're not going anywhere, Bobby."

"But—"

"Don't even think about it," he warned.

There was no way I was getting past him. Sheriff Mustache was too big, too strong and too angry. Getting into the Big Dance would be impossible.

Until *a-choooooooo!* Gramps sneezed into Mr. Summers's face.

A hurricane of spit showered Sheriff Mustache's mustache. Pieces of semi-chewed jelly beans stuck to my math teacher's face.

"Eewww," he groaned.

Gramps gave me a nudge as if to say *go!* I saw my chance and dashed inside.

"Allison!" I called out. "Wait!"

My sneakers squeaked as I ran across the hardwood floor. The lights were faded inside the gym. The place had been decorated with streamers, banners and a few disco balls to give it the feel of a real dance club.

I finally caught up to Allison. She wore a silver and blue dress with black shoes and a sparkly headband.

She looked amazing!

But her outfit didn't match her mood at all. Clearly, Allison was annoyed at having to come to the Big Dance.

And she was steaming mad at me.

"I don't want to speak to you, Bobby. Ever!"

She crossed her arms. It wasn't two seconds before Sheriff Mustache rushed up, grabbing me from behind.

"Let's go, Bobby," he said. "Out! And come Monday, it's straight to Vice Principal Hildge."

Mr. Summers grabbed my shirt collar. Kids all around us had been grooving to the music, laughing and chatting, but when they saw how mad Sheriff Mustache was, a few of them looked over.

"But," I said, trying to squirm out of his grip, "with all due respect, sir, I did pay for a ticket."

"I don't care what you think you did," he said to me. "You are out of here right now!"

"What do you mean, you paid for a ticket?" Allison asked.

"Like I said, I paid for a ticket," I told her. "Okay, yes. I went into the green envelope and took two tickets, but I did pay for them."

"You paid for them?" Allison asked. "How?"

People started gathering around because of all the commotion. Seeing my friends—well, my old friends—and other kids my age wearing ties always looked weird to me. But that would have been me if it weren't for Sheriff Mustache in the first place. I tried again to squiggle out of his grip, but it was too tight.

"I put cash in the envelope," I said.

"You put cash, you mean you put money, in the envelope?" Allison said.

"Uh-huh. The full amount."

Allison looked up at her father.

"You told me he stole them."

"He did. He came into my house and took them without permission," Sheriff Mustache replied. "Let's go, Connor. Out. Now."

"No, you said he *stole* them."

"Don't get technical with me, Allison," Sheriff Mustache answered. "What he did was wrong."

190

"But he didn't steal them. You made it sound like he took them without paying for them."

"Not now, Allison."

"Yes now, Dad," she replied. Allison crossed her arms, a look of fierce determination on her face. The disco ball caused all sorts of sparkles to dance across her dress. "It's like you hate him or something."

"I don't *hate* any of my students," Sheriff Mustache said, as if it were the most preposterous thing he'd ever heard.

"Okay, fine," Allison answered. The circle of people grew bigger. My sister and Finkelstein walked up. "Then tell me why you strongly, strongly, strongly dislike Bobby?"

Allison recrossed her arms and waited for an answer. About forty kids waited for his response, too. Even the music had stopped.

"Okay, you want to know why?" Sheriff Mustache said, finally letting me go. "Because I like order. I like neatness. I like A to lead to B and then B to lead to C, but you're one of those kids," he said, pointing at me. "With you, A leads to Z, which leads to X and then to D. I don't like that. I don't like that at all and I certainly don't want that for my daughter."

It got eerily quiet. The kids surrounding us dared not move. A part of me felt like I should defend myself, like I should speak up and maybe call him a total unfair jerk or something. But another part of me felt like, "What's the point?" I mean, like it or not, this was still Allison's dad—and my math teacher— and insulting him, I knew, wasn't gonna get me any- where.

"Dad, what are you talking about?" Allison said, her green eyes lasered in on her father.

"Oh, I know his type. I mean I've been around middle school boys a long time, Allison, and I don't like the way that this one is sniffing around you at all." Sheriff Mustache pointed at me. "Ask Mrs. Mank, his old math teacher. Bobby's one of those kids who thinks with his pants instead of his brain."

"With all due respect, sir," I said softly. "When it comes to your daughter, I think the real problem is I think with my heart."

The girls who were watching us said "Awww." My stomach fluttered.

"I didn't mean to cause any trouble tonight," I said to Allison. "I just wanted to tell you that, well, I was sorry and that you mean a lot to me. And I feel bad that I caused your dad to get so mad at you and lose trust in you 'cause really, you didn't do anything. You didn't do anything at all." I turned to Sheriff Mustache. "It's the truth. She didn't do anything."

Sheriff Mustache looked around at all the people watching.

"Bye, Allison," I said. "Come on, Gramps. Let's go."

I took a step forward and the crowd parted. All the kids, dressed in their fancy clothes, wearing either too much makeup or too much cologne, were quiet and subdued. Gramps followed. I knew he wanted to say something, to really rip into Sheriff Mustache, but instead he kept his mouth shut, letting me fight my own battles in my own way.

That was kinda cool of him.

"Nice going, Dad," Allison said.

"I don't know why any of this is my fault," Sheriff Mustache replied. "I already sold him two tickets. Why don't you explain to us what happened to those, Bobby?"

I stopped.

"Yeah, Mr. Smart Guy," Sheriff Mustache said. "Where's your answer for that?"

I looked at Allison. "I wasn't gonna tell."

"Tell what?" she asked.

"He wouldn't let me buy four tickets," I explained.

"So?" Allison said. "Where are these two tickets you bought?"

"I gave 'em to them," I said, nudging at Finkelstein and Hill.

"To us?" Hill and Finkelstein said at practically the same time.

I nodded, but Hill didn't get it.

"You bought my ticket?" she asked.

"I knew how much you wanted to go." Hill looked nice in her fancy dress, I thought. Happy. "I felt bad for you. I mean, I guess I was just trying to, you know, make up for not being a good broth . . . I mean, buddy."

She stood there completely frozen.

"And you, like, bought my ticket, too?" Finkelstein asked.

"Yeah, well," I answered, "that's what friends do, I guess."

"Friends?" Finkelstein said, looking for more.

"Okay," I replied. "Best friends."

A giant smile spread across his face.

"He-hurrggh, he-hurrggh." Finkelstein rushed forward and gave me a huge hug.

"I knew you loved me, Bobby."

"Get off of me, Finkelstein." I pushed him away. "And, by the way, dots and stripes are the stupidest combination I have ever seen on another human being's teeth."

"I just have one word for ya, Bobby," Finkelstein answered, flashing every tooth in his mouth. *"Sexxxxxyy."*

I couldn't help but smile. "You're a moron."

"He-hurrggh, he-hurrggh."

"Wait a minute!" Hill said, suddenly figuring it out. "You mean metal mouth is supposed to be my Secret Someone?"

"And I'm supposed to be here with stick girl?" Finkelstein replied.

"Magnet face."

"Ping-Pong table chest."

"Bicycle cable lips!"

"String-bean Sally!"

"Will you two shut up?" I said. *"Jeez!* Yes, you're here together," I told them. "I mean it's like so obvious that the two of you have a huge crush on each other, so gimme a break already, would ya?"

"We do?" Finkelstein asked, looking over at Hill.

"Finkelstein, go dance with your date," I said, pushing him toward my sister. Finkelstein was the only kid in the entire gymnasium wearing a bow tie. And no, he didn't look good in it. "Trust me," I said to him, "her heart is playing hopscotch in her chest right now."

Just then, Finkelstein and Hill got all googly-eyed with each other and the fireworks went off, like in some sort of bad, cheesy, make-you-want-to-vomit movie.

195

"Bobby," Hill said, smoothing out her yellow dress.

"Yeah."

"Thanks."

She smiled. It wasn't a big smile, but it was the kind that told me that we were good once again. All was forgiven.

I smiled back.

"May I pleeeze hav za pleasure of zis dance, Madame?" Finkelstein said in a fake French accent.

"Don't mind if I do." Hill did one of those curtsy things.

"He-hurrggh, he-hurrggh."

"Is that how you always laugh?" Hill asked.

"Yeah, why, you don't like it?"

"No," she said to Finkelstein. "Actually, I think it's kind of . . . well, *sexxxy*."

Finkelstein's face beamed with joy. The disco lights then hit his teeth, making every piece of metal in his mouth glitter like a striped and dotted asteroid belt.

"He-hurrggh, he-hurrggh."

The whole thing made me wanna puke.

"Come on, Gramps," I said, beginning to walk off. "Let's go." The circle broke apart and people began heading back to the dance floor, the refreshment bar and the tables covered in spill-resistant purple plastic.

It took no time for the sound of chatter and laughter to refill the air. Our little show was over.

Suddenly, someone grabbed my shoulder and turned me around.

"Why didn't you just tell me, Bobby?" asked Allison. "I mean, I could have bought the tickets."

"'Cause, you know," I said. "Good deeds should be done for the sake of doing them, not for the credit." Once again, I realized how out of place my clothes were for a formal party. Jeans and a T-shirt, just like I would wear on any other Friday night at the mall, while Allison looked like a million dollars that had just come off the printing press.

Maybe my father was right. Second-class guys chasing first-class girls, it was a recipe for nothing but heartache.

"I'm sorry I ruined your evening," I said, apologizing again.

"You didn't ruin it, Bobby. You made it perfect."

My heart jumped. *I did?*

Allison smiled at me with a zillion watts of super-teeth, and a grin spread across my face. She then led me out onto the dance floor.

"Move aside, Daddy!" she ordered Sheriff Mustache. "I want to dance with my date."

He looked at our hands, our fingers interlocked. Sheriff Mustache didn't budge.

"I said *move,*" Allison said, pushing past him. "I'm not a little girl, you know."

"But—"

"Don't say another word," she snapped at her father. "We will talk about this later when we get home."

Sheriff Mustache thought about it for a moment, then stepped aside.

"Wait!" I said. "Hill," I called out. "Where's that thing I gave you?"

"What thing?" she answered.

"Where's the envelope I gave you?"

"This?" she said, pulling it out of her silver purse. "It's right here."

"What's that?" Allison asked.

"It's . . ." I stopped. "It's for my grandfather."

I let go of Allison's hand and dashed up to Gramps.

"Here." I handed him the envelope. "I don't think I'm going to need this. But you might." I handed him the keys to the car. "Go get her, Gramps. Go get the girl you love."

A big, yellow-toothed grin spread across Gramps's face.

"Shall we?" I asked, walking back up to Allison.

"Lead the way," she replied.

Before we got to the dance floor, I heard Gramps say to Sheriff Mustache, "You know they're gonna make out hot and heavy later tonight, right?"

"You do realize that this is my daughter you're talking about, don't you?" Sheriff Mustache answered.

"Well, I hate to tell you this," Gramps responded, "but she's a tamale."

Sheriff Mustache straightened his tie and brushed out an imaginary wrinkle from his jacket, trying to regain the look of a man in a position of authority.

"Do you have a ticket?" he asked in a formal way.

"Sure you don't want a jelly bean?" Gramps replied. "How 'bout a tangy tangerine?"

We stepped onto the dance floor with perfect timing, because just then the DJ made an announcement. "This next song is for couples only."

My heart flapped like a bluebird soaring through the sky. This was the reason every kid went to these crazy things anyway.

But then tragedy struck. And not from the center of my pants.

Thank goodness, too. I mean how in the world was I going to do a slow dance with Allison while sporting vicious wood?

Nope, it was a different disaster: Nathan Ox.

"Well, if it isn't boner boy Bobby Connor. Hey Bobby, in baseball, a pitcher can throw strikes or they can throw . . ."

Nathan wound up to bash me in my egg basket. And I could tell this was gonna be a big one, the kind that sent your pistachios into your throat. But Allison jumped in front of Nathan.

"You touch him," Allison said, "and I will tell every person at this school that you are so lame you had to buy your own ticket to the Big Dance and pretend that it was given to you by a Secret Someone because you're such a loser that you knew no one would ever want to be here with you."

Terror crossed Nathan's face.

"That's right," Allison informed him. "The ticket seller's daughter knows a few little secrets, doesn't she?"

"You wouldn't," Nathan said.

"Oh yes I would," Allison replied. "I'll even go grab the microphone and make an announcement over the PA right now."

Allison's green eyes blazed. Wow, clearly she was a woman not to be messed with.

It took Nathan all of three seconds to see that Allison was a hundred percent serious. And if she did make that kind of announcement over the microphone, it could be the most embarrassing middle school moment ever in the history of our school.

Well, the second most embarrassing moment. I'd probably always hold the number one spot for all time.

"What's the matter, Bobby?" Nathan said to me in a sarcastic tone. "You need your girlfriend to save you?"

My girlfriend? Wow, I sure liked the sound of that.

"Yep, I do," I said, smiling. "I sure do. Now if you'll excuse us, Nathan," I said as we walked around him, "it's time for those of us with dates to go hit the dance floor. It's kind of a couples-only thing."

Both Allison and I laughed, then we headed hand in hand for the middle of the gymnasium. She'd fixed it so that Nathan would never mess with me again.

Well, never is a long time. But at least he'd leave me alone for a little bit.

Though it was my first time ever slow dancing with a girl, I swayed back and forth with ease. Something about Allison just made things in my life work.

"For a while," I said, "I really thought this night was never going to happen."

"Because of my dad?" she asked.

"Your dad? Nuh-uh," I answered. "Because of the CIA. Appears there's been a break-in down at the Pentagon and the Navy SEALs are stumped."

"The Navy SEALs?" she said.

"It's a black ops thing. My lips are supposed to be sealed."

"Sealed, huh?"

"Yeah," I answered. "And really, with all the secrets I hold with these lips, I think there's only one true way for me to ensure that democracy continues to exist in the United States of America."

"Oh, there is, is there?" Allison said with a gleam in her eye.

"Most definitely," I said. "For the security of our country, of course."

"Of course," she answered.

I leaned in and closed my eyes. This was going to be a magical first kiss, the kind most people only dreamed about. After all, the lighting was soft, the music was smooth, and best of all, the girl was, well . . . first-class. Nothing could stop me now.

Except for the sudden explosion in my ear.

"He-hurrggh, he-hurrggh!"

My eyes flew open.

"Dude, I just totally made out with your sister!"

"Shut up, Finkelstein!"

"Like, does it weird you out that your best friend is completely swapping spit-ola with your baby sis?"

he asked. "I mean, that's just gotta be kinda freaky-deaky, right?"

"Can we not talk about this right now, Finkelstein?" I said. "I'm kinda busy here."

"Gotcha, bro," he answered. "But just so you know, when she gets back from the bathroom, I'm totally going back for more than just tongue. This time, I'm going for esophagus!"

Finkelstein, his braces glittering underneath the lights of the disco ball, darted away.

"Now," I said, face-to-face with Allison again. "Where were we?"

"National security," she answered.

"Oh, right. The safety of our country."

She closed her eyes, I closed mine, and like in a Hollywood blockbuster when the hero finally gets the girl at the end, we kissed.

Magic!

21

Two Minus One Does Not Make One: A Math Poem from My Heart

Two Minus One Does Not Make One
The Sum
No matter how you do the math,
When you take the two of us
And subtract you
Leaves a less complete me.

Two Minus One Does Not Make One
The Fun
No matter how much glee
When you are not with me
Is less.

Two Minus One Does Not Make One
The Joy
In this boy

Is dead without you
And I'd do anything to win you back.

Two Minus One Does Not Make One
The Rhymes don't matter
The pain just splatters
And splatters and splatters my soul
Because you are not in my life.

Two Minus One Does Not Make One
But one plus one
Like me and you
Equals more than two
It adds up to . . .
Forever.

I got an A when I read that poem out loud for English class. But better than that was the kiss I got in the hallway once class let out. Allison practically smooched my lips off.

"I told ya, Bobby," Finkelstein said later that night as he put another scoop of homemade candied yams on his dinner plate, "chicks dig poetry."

"They sure do, Alfred," Gramps said. "They sure do." Gramps turned to his left. "Can I get you more green beans, dear?"

"No, thanks," Grandma said.

"How about a bit more meat loaf?" Gramps offered. "Would you like just a wee bit more? There's sweet potatoes, too, honey."

"I'm good, dear. I'm perfectly good," my grandmother answered.

"You know, he hasn't cooked me a meal since nineteen eighty-one," she said, turning to me. Gram had blue eyes with wrinkles around the edges, but whenever she looked at me, I always saw a fiery lady who still had some pop. She wasn't some kind of old woman ready for a museum. My gram had spunk.

Then again, I guess she had to in order to live with Gramps for all those years.

"To tell you the truth, I thought he only ate jelly beans," I said. We all laughed.

I looked around at the dinner table. Me, Finkelstein, Hill and Allison all greatly enjoyed watching Gramps play the role of a generous and gracious dinner host.

Too bad Dad and Mom weren't invited. But I don't think they would have accepted Gramps's invitation anyway. They were still mad, especially because Gramps refused to apologize or pay to get the garage door fixed. He thought the episode the other night was some of the best decision-making he'd made in years and he wasn't gonna budge an inch.

"Aw, poopy-pants!" Gramps suddenly shouted, remembering something. "The pie is still in the oven."

Then, wearing his cooking apron, Gramps disappeared into the kitchen to go make sure he didn't burn our dessert.

As soon as he left the room, Gram leaned over and put her hand on mine in that grandmotherly type of way. "I know you wrote the poem, Bobby," she whispered so that no one else could hear.

"You do?" I said.

"Uh-huh," she replied. "I do." Gram checked to see that the others weren't listening.

They weren't. They were all too busy staring at Finkelstein as he explained the psychological theory behind his new set of braces. Today's color: pitch-black.

"See, it's like a mouth of infinite mystery," he told them.

I shook my head. *What a moron.*

"So how'd he win you back, Gram?" I asked. "He told me he read you the poem and that it worked like a charm."

"Farts," she replied.

I almost choked on my food.

"What?"

"I knew he wasn't the author of that poem," she said. "It was too good."

She took a sip of water and wiped her chin with a napkin.

"But then he promised not to blow me out from under the covers anymore with gas," she added. "Do you know how many years I've had to deal with him tooting his butt trumpet at full volume?"

I laughed.

"I know it sounds weird, but really, it's about respect, Bobby," Gram said. "I needed to know that he still respected and cared about me. Relationships don't survive without respect, care and trust."

"Trust?" I said, looking at Allison. Finkelstein had his mouth open big enough to swallow a chair. Hill and Allison peeked inside, inspecting the metallic architectural wonder that was Finkelstein's latest brace-face adventure.

"Trust, Bobby," Gram continued, "might actually be the most important ingredient of them all."

I caught Allison's eye and we grinned at each other. Then Gramps came into the room carrying a piping hot pie, fresh out of the oven.

"Who's ready for dessert?" he asked in a big, excited voice. "It's boysenberry!"

Hill's jaw practically dropped.

"Just kidding," Gramps said to my sister. "It's apple. Just good ol' fashioned apple pie."

Hill laughed. Yep, Gramps was a wacko, but he could also be one heck of a sweet guy, too.

It was a fun night, and life, I had to admit, was finally good. Even if I did have to go back to correctional erectional therapy the following Tuesday.

Dr. Cox, however, had flown the coop. When I showed up at her office, that's when they broke the news to me.

She'd vanished. Maybe to Africa? Maybe to Argentina? No one knew for sure. But she left a note that I was allowed to see.

Moved to a country that starts with an A. Need to resolve some feelings about yellow dolls. Throw out whatever supplies you don't want to keep because I am not returning till the hair on my head grows back to at least shoulder length. I shaved it as a symbol of starting new.

The bad news, however, was the last part.

P.S. Change the air-conditioning filters because I think there are dust mites in the air, there's a

virus on the computer and Bobby Connor still
owes this school eighteen hours of therapy.

Ah jeez, is she serious?

In fact, that's what I told my new therapist.

"Ah jeez, is she serious?"

"I'm afraid she is," said the lady standing in front of me. A moment later, she stretched out her hand.

"I'm Mrs. Roberts, the new school guidance counselor." Mrs. Roberts looked more like somebody's aunt than she did a psychologist. She had shoulder-length brown hair, fingernails painted red, and ruby earrings and necklace.

"Hey," I grunted.

"Is something wrong?" she asked. "You seem a little upset."

"Well, wouldn't you be?" I said. "I mean how long will it be before you ask me if that telephone reminds me of a ding-dong?"

"Excuse me?"

"Or maybe you have a shopping bag full of vegetables underneath your desk and you want me to identify all the perverted pieces of cucumber."

"Bobby," she said. "You have me all wrong."

"I do?" I said. "Are you telling me that all people

like you aren't twisted freakazoids who see ding-a-lings in trees and museum paintings and armrests?"

"Armrests?"

"Yeah, armrests," I said. "I mean I'm just a normal kid. Why is that so hard for you people to see?"

"I agree," she answered.

"You . . . what?"

"I agree," she repeated. Her voice was calm and even. "I read your file, looked at your grades, talked to your teachers and have come to the conclusion that, yep, you seem pretty normal."

"I do?" I was still waiting to be asked about something wacky like lamps that looked like nakedness.

Mrs. Roberts smiled again.

"Yep, more or less normal," she said. "It's just puberty, Bobby. That's all it is. And every young boy and every young girl in this world goes through it."

"So what's the, you know," I asked, sort of looking down at my pants. "The solution?"

"Solution? There's no 'solution,'" she replied. I dropped my head in despair. "But there's nothing wrong with you, either. At least nothing that requires counseling, as far as I can see."

"So, um . . . ," I said. "Why am I here?"

"I really don't know," she answered. "Unless, of

course, there's something that you do want to talk about?"

"Uh, not really."

"Okay," Mrs. Roberts said. "Fine. But if you change your mind, just let me know, okay? I'll be the permanent replacement here."

She scribbled down a few notes in a thin black leather notebook, but I couldn't see what she was writing.

"So, that's it?" I said. "I can go?"

"Well, we still have to figure out a way for you to get credit for those eighteen hours you owe," she told me. "I talked to the vice principal, but I can't get you off the hook for those."

"I knew it," I said. "I knew there was a catch."

"Slow down, Bobby, we have some options," she replied. "Option one, we can continue therapy."

"No way, *bzzpt*," I said. "What's option two?"

"You can transfer to another school," she offered. "I can make the paperwork read so that it doesn't look like an expulsion."

And leave Allison. No way!

"And option three?" I asked. I was expecting I'd have to stand with no clothes on in the middle of the playground or something.

"You can write your story."

"Write my story?" I said. "I don't know what that means."

"Well," she explained after pausing to make another notation in her leather book, "it seems to me you have had quite a saga as of late. Why don't you write your adventure, turn it in to me and I'll consider that good enough to cancel out the rest of the therapy hours you owe to the school."

"You can do that?" I asked.

She nodded. Her smile was warm.

I thought about it for a moment.

"Just write my adventure and that's it?" I said. "And I can go?"

"Yes, Bobby, you can go," she replied. "Of course, you might just find that writing all about it helps, too. Sort of a way to get it all out of your system, if you know what I mean."

I decided to go for option three and ya know what? My new therapist was right. It did sorta get it all out of my system.

Except for my boners. I still get about eighteen weenie pipes a day.

Some things, I guess, I'll just never understand.

ACKNOWLEDGMENTS

With great appreciation to the incomparable Al Zuckerman, who supported this project from the moment it "popped up," and the fantastic Stacey Barney, who has now endured—and unintentionally created—more penis puns than any editor should ever have to endure . . . and done so with a smile at every juncture of the journey.